GABRIELLE MARIE KOZAK

Life or Death

an ancient legend

"No, life cannot die! No matter how dark it is,
I will not let it die!
"There is Hope still! There is Light, there is
Life! There is always something to hope for!
To live for!
"I will not let it die!"

— Aura Eienno

Contents

Foreword

Dear Reader,

I wrote this short story during five days of deep depression as a seventeen-year-old.

I polished it at twenty—

because, though I no longer have to convince myself to hope,

there may always be others who do.

This book is for you.

God bless and Mary keep you,
Gabrielle Marie Kozak

Acknowledgments

I would like to acknowledge and thank those who have been the smaller Lights in my own life.

And all those who provide that light to others.

Thank you…

and I hope this book can be yours.

I

"I will give you a great Power. It is not only power: it is a risk. You can use it wisely or you can use it foolishly. The choice is yours. And this Power, the greatest of all, is called Hope, or Light.

"But for you, there will be no risk, for your path is already set out for you. You will walk in the darkness and there will never be light. For in you is created, not Hope, but Despair. Not Light, but Darkness.

"We shall see which is the strongest Power—Hope or Despair? Light or Darkness? Life or Death?"

Two

Dark Aura

I T WAS RAINING. It was always raining, thought Aura to herself gloomily; more especially when Aura felt like raining herself, and most especially when she had to go to school instead.

"I'm a time traveler," her friend Eva had joked with her the day before as they finished the walk together. "And so are you. When will we go to?"

It hadn't been raining that day, Aura thought to herself, semi-consolingly.

"How about the beginning of the world?" she had decided. "I want to see everything clean and beautiful and—alive."

Her friend had pulled a face. "Really, Aura? But what to expect. I'm going to take a tally at lunch today!"

But of course, Aura remembered. Eva was that type of person, always looking to attract attention and make friends. Aura herself was lucky to be one of those—she suspected it was merely because their walks to school often aligned. The two didn't even sit close to each other during class.

Aura told herself fiercely she didn't care.

She was nearing the corner, she realized—the corner where Eva was always waiting for her. But this time there was no sign of her taller, popular friend.

Aura's eyes widened in surprise. Eva must be sick.

What a coincidence, since Aura herself had felt sick this morning. But her foster mother had insisted she go to school anyway.

Aura bit her lip. She knew her foster mother didn't like her, and neither had her real mother.

Aura knew that because the last memory she had of her was her mother holding her up and looking dimly into the baby's eyes. Looking at her for the first time. And the baby had been screaming.

"What is there to hope for?"

Then she had dropped her head back, and died—leaving Aura and her twin sister alone in the world, since no one had ever located their father.

Yes, there had been a twin sister, until she died as well, only a few hours after their mother. Aura remembered her as well. She could never understand her feelings when she thought about that sister who hadn't survived. She only knew that there had always been a spark of something between the two. Not hatred, not anger… Something above either of those, above any and every emotion that had a name. The closest Aura could think of was a kind of fatalistic antagonism. As if they had been born to be enemies. And on Aura's side, a trace of terrifying horror towards her sister. Aura shivered to remember it, vague as her memories were.

Memories that shouldn't have existed in the first place. Not from when she was so young.

But they did.

She passed the corner and marched on resolutely. Perhaps the fact that Eva wasn't going to school today would mean that Aura would arrive there early, as Eva always wanted to talk and that slowed both of them down. But when she was alone, her thoughts flew as fast as Eva's tongue.

Oh, yes, she remembered her twin. She remembered that they had been very different. Both their hair had been dark, but Aura's was more of rich brown, while her sister's had been an overwhelmingly dark black. Aura's eyes were, incidentally, a deep, shining red, which perhaps contributed to the aura of unapproachable mystery about her. Her twin's had been some kind of luminous, cold blueish-purple. Aura's red eyes had become more dull and less noticeable over time, thankfully.

Aura sighed, just thinking about her eyes. She was sure that was part of why no one wanted to be seen with her, not even her friend. She was generally accepted as 'weird' around all those who knew her—that is, if they even knew her name. Their teachers didn't call her out often, just mostly when she was late or not paying attention, which amounted to the same thing.

Now she was approaching the school building itself, almost half an hour early. Aura always got to school in plenty of time, though not usually this early. And definitely no one else would be arriving this early. Aura slowly tramped up the front steps. She had just resigned herself to sitting alone for an entire thirty minutes when she saw the girl.

Aura knew right away that she was a new girl—probably a transfer student, since the school year was already a few months in and it was almost winter. The girl's back was turned to her, and she was wearing the ordinary junior-student uniform, just like Aura, but the girl's short, straight hair was a crisp, pitch black Aura had never seen before.

Somehow Aura was filled with a sixth sense of apprehension as the girl heard her footsteps and turned to face her, still sitting on the bench. Aura stood still, her hands frozen on her backpack straps as she watched.

The girl had longish bangs, that reached almost to her eyes. Her eyes in themselves were striking: a light purple. She stared back at Aura nonchalantly; and then, suddenly, she smiled.

"Hi." Her voice was quiet and unobtrusive, but somehow it sent a thrill of something like terror through Aura, and she started.

"Hello," she managed to reply, her mind whirling. "Are you new?" It sounded stupid, but it was all Aura could think of at the time.

Slowly her nerves calmed as Aura told herself there was absolutely no reason to be freaking out. This girl looked friendly, didn't she?

"Yeah, I think I am. Have we met before?" the girl added, her purple eyes searchingly pensive. "My name is Kaja."

"No, I don't think we have." It took Aura a moment to realize Kaja was holding out her hand, and quickly she followed her example, shaking the girl's hand timidly at first and then energetically as Kaja set the lead.

Mentally, Aura laughed at herself, taking a deep breath and smiling back at Kaja. Why had she thought Kaja's hand would be cold and unnatural? It was just as warm as her own. And Kaja was simply a nice girl. Aura was just a pathetic coward, like everyone said. But, Kaja didn't know that—yet.

"My name's Aura. Where are you from?" Aura ventured hopefully.

Kaja merely shrugged. "Taimoni," she supplied, referring to a distant province in that country. "How are you?"

Aura blinked. No one ever asked her that question.

"I—I feel great," she replied, and somehow it suddenly became true, though she still had a horrible feeling in her stomach that just wouldn't go away. "How about you?"

And then Kaja smiled again. It was just another ordinary, friendly smile—it could only be, of course—but something about it sent chills down Aura's spine.

"You'll see."

The half hour passed, bringing in its wake the beginning of classes for the day. The other students arrived one after another, and gradually Aura ended up in her usual loner spot: the bench nearest to the school doors. Kaja was claimed by some other, more popular girls, a few of whom seemed hesitant at first, almost like Aura, but who soon got over their apprehensions.

Aura sat alone, still wearing her backpack, staring at the ground of the school veranda and the soles of her classmates' shoes. She pulled her school blazer tighter about her, feeling chilly. With the return of the cold, her chaotic thoughts returned as well, in greater force. She shivered.

What was it about Kaja that frightened her? Aura didn't want to admit that she was frightened, but that was the closest word for what she was feeling. Fright and horror. The kind of horror that made her never want to see Kaja's face again. But one principle of Aura's was that she always face her fears, and as she remembered that she forced herself to look up.

Her red eyes glanced over the crowds of talking high school girls, and then she spotted her. It wasn't hard. Kaja's incredibly black hair would have stood out anywhere. But she wasn't facing Aura, and Aura focused her gaze on the back of Kaja's head, ignoring the fact that anyone who saw her would consider her even weirder than she was.

And suddenly Kaja wheeled around swiftly, as if she had sensed Aura's eyes on her. She only glanced her way a moment, but Aura tensed—for a moment she fancied that Kaja's eyes were actually alight, and that her mouth was curved into a knowing smirk. But of course that was just Aura's imagination. The next instant she turned away from Kaja again, but the damage had been done.

Aura half-stood up, her pulse racing. She knew where she had seen luminous purple eyes like those before—her twin sister.

She tried to calm herself. Her twin sister was dead, and besides, Kaja's eyes were perfectly normal, as normal as purple eyes could get. And no, she hadn't smirked at Aura. Why would she have?

But still the memory bothered Aura all throughout classes that day, and for the entire walk home as well. Her steps were slow and as she approached the shabby, small home in the suburbs that she and her foster parents lived in, she realized she was more than ten minutes later than she usually was. She ought to have dinner started by now, and her foster mother would have come back from work and be annoyed that Aura wasn't home yet.

Aura looked up at the forbidding door and shrugged her shoulders, reluctantly lifting her hand to open the door and let herself in. Face your fears, she told herself, with an attempt at a smile.

"I'm home!" she called out, stepping into the front hallway. She closed the door behind her, and then stopped. The lights were off.

Her foster mother hadn't come home yet. She must have forgotten to lock the door when she left for work this morning.

With a real smile this time, Aura quickly slipped into her room, leaving her backpack behind on her bed and running into the kitchen. She was just lucky today, if her foster mother was late. With the agility and speed of long practice, Aura began a pot of water boiling on the stove, started the oven heating, and then collected dishes from the cabinets to bring into the dining room.

Her hands were full, so she bumped the old-fashioned light switch with her forehead, and the light over the table flickered on. But right away Aura stopped, sensing in the dark atmosphere of the room that something was wrong.

Slowly she set the dishes on the table—and then she saw for the first time the bloody hand print on the far edge of the table. For a moment Aura was positive her heart had stopped, but then a kind of overwhelming calm came over her, and she walked slowly around the table.

She knew what she was going to see even before she saw it. Her foster mother was there, on the floor, covered in blood and obviously dead, even if only for a few minutes. Aura realized that and she felt a cold shudder. The murderer could not be far away.

For a moment her legs were frozen, but then she found she could run, and so she did, out of the house and down the street to the police station.

She was horrified to find that she felt somehow cold and emotionless. She had not loved her foster mother, but neither had she hated her, and the entire thing was a horrible shock. And before her eyes was continually the image of blood.

What Aura didn't realize at the time was that her eyes were that same color.

She ran into the police station, and gasped out four words. "There's been a murder!"

Some hours later, Aura was finally alone, alone to think and ponder over that horrible day's events. She had had the opportunity to collect a suitcase of her belongings from her old room, and right now she was in a room of a nearby orphanage. She would be having roommates, but they hadn't gone to bed yet, and there was no one else in the room. It was dark—Aura hadn't bothered to turn on the lights.

The police had come to inspect the crime scene, but hadn't come to any definite conclusions about who had done it. Aura was aware that she herself was a suspect, but she didn't care about that, at least not yet. She was still numb from shock. Only about an hour after she'd discovered her foster mother's body came the news that her foster father had been brutally murdered on his way home from work. He had been kind to Aura sometimes, and she knew she was going to miss him. But she couldn't shake off the unreal feeling, that none of this was real, she was only dreaming, it was all a nightmare, and she would wake up soon.

She hadn't needed an entire suitcase for her belongings. Just a bag with a change of clothes, and her photo of her parents that she'd always had. She liked to look at it, especially when she was feeling down, and she looked at it now, touching the worn wooden frame gently. She knew the entire photo by heart, but she didn't often study her mother's face. She had been pretty—golden haired and nothing like Aura—but Aura knew and remembered that her real mother had not wanted her.

But her father—Aura liked to look at him. He was tall, with dark brown hair much like her own, and bright green eyes that seemed to have traces of Aura's childhood eyes' luminosity. He smiled and looked at the camera as if he was completely happy, yet seriously as if he had real purpose in life and knew it. Confident, optimistic, cheery. Aura knew she would recognize him instantly if she ever ran into him. Which, of course, would never happen. She had never seen him in person and there was no chance of it happening in the future.

Yet, now, as she stared at his picture, she could remember there having been something close to her real father's spirit in her foster father's eyes, and Aura found that she could cry for him. For both of them.

Cold and meaningless as her lonely life was, she was mildly surprised to find she could still feel emotion. Sorrow and pain.

Why? Didn't she have enough of that already?

But still she cried.

It was still raining outside. Raining, and she was raining as well. Aura was alone again, as she had been as a baby and a very small child; alone in a world she knew hated and despised her.

Everything was darkness. There was no light.

Three

II

That was what was said, in the moment the greater Light was created. With the Light was created also Darkness. Light is nothing without Darkness. And Darkness is everything without Light.

A world was created, a world with both Light and Darkness. They mixed, and became lost in a powerless gray. Gray overtook everything, but gray is neither Light nor Darkness, and a brighter Light was needed. A Light that would shine strong and outshine the gray. A Light that would shine forever and turn the gray to white. For Light is Hope, and Life.

But when that brighter Light was created, so was a darker Darkness, and these were two colors that could not merge. They could only attempt to wipe each other out, leaving the world either in Light or in Darkness, whichever would survive the battle.

Four

One Month Later

⁂

SHE WAS WALKING to school alone. She had not always walked to school alone, but today was different. Today was a new day in a new city for her, and Jadelyn wasn't sure if she liked it.

She was from a nearby city, but her family had had to move for her father to keep his job. The city they were from had been smaller, and Jadelyn had gone to the same school as both her younger siblings, but in this city she would be going to the province girls' high school, and since she was the only child in her family that was high school-age, she'd be going alone.

Jadelyn wondered boredly if she was going to like going to school without her siblings' being within a one-mile radius. And, to be honest, she had to admit she didn't know. But she had hopes. It probably helped that she and her younger sister had gotten into a huge argument only the night before about who got which bed. But Jadelyn had won the top bunk, since she was older.

She smiled at the memory of her little sister's sulky face. Stacie was always cute, but most especially when she was angry.

So this is the school, she thought to herself as she glanced up at the large, somewhat imposing building some minutes after she had begun walking. It was just as big as the school for all grades back in her home city, if not even bigger. In the front was a large, roofed veranda where crowds of girls her age were talking.

Good, so she wasn't late.

Jadelyn leapt lightly up the steps, her long, slightly dark brown hair flowing out behind her and shining in the morning sunlight. No one noticed her at first—Jadelyn was glad. Taking a closer look, she came to realize that a lot of them were gathered around one person. Jadelyn stood on her tip-toes and caught her first glimpse of who she vaguely assumed to be the most popular girl in school.

Even if the girl was obviously popular, there was something about her that set Jadelyn off from the first.

She scowled to herself. She shouldn't judge.

The girl wasn't completely normal—besides beautiful, short, straight ebony-black hair, she had light purple eyes. But her smile was warm and friendly, even if not aimed at Jadelyn personally. Jadelyn mentally chided herself for being suspicious. Whoever that junior student was, she was definitely someone to know if Jadelyn wanted to make friends.

But Jadelyn wasn't going to try to approach her yet, not in the first minutes of her first day. She glanced towards the large entrance to the main school building, starting when she realized that the girl sitting on the bench there was studying her quite interestedly. Jadelyn stared back frankly, noting that her previously unnoticed watcher had dark red eyes—the color of blood—and dark hair, long like Jadelyn's.

She looked lonely. Jadelyn smiled as she walked over.

"Hi, I'm Jadelyn," she introduced herself.

The girl stood up, still clutching the straps of her backpack.

"Welcome to Coloni High," she returned, and finally smiled back—a sad sort of smile, Jadelyn thought to herself. "I'm Aura."

"That's a nice name," Jadelyn told her without really thinking. But the girl's eyes lit up.

"Thanks." Now she really smiled. "So is Jadelyn."

"You can call me Jade," Jadelyn laughed. "Have you been at this school all your life? I mean, your high school life?" she corrected herself hastily.

"Yeah." Aura laughed too, but Jadelyn got the impression she wasn't in the practice of laughing. "I…I hope you like it here," Aura added, to break the suddenly awkward silence.

Jadelyn's blue eyes sparkled. "I'm sure I will," she agreed emphatically.

Suddenly someone came running up the steps behind Jadelyn, nearly running into the new girl. "Aura—oop, sorry!" the girl blurted out as Jadelyn jumped aside, somewhat startled, to find a golden-haired high school junior behind her.

"Hey, Aura, who's your new friend?" the girl demanded instantly. Jadelyn couldn't help but notice that Aura looked somewhat flustered.

"Hi Eva… She's Jadelyn," Aura replied, half an instant later. "A new girl—"

"Hi Jadelyn!" Eva beamed, fairly taking Jadelyn's hand and pulling her off. "Have you met Kaja yet? She arrived only a month ago, and everyone has to know her! Her style is just…"

Eva's voice trailed away as she brought Jadelyn to meet Kaja.

Aura watched them go as she pulled her blazer tighter. It was even colder now than it had been a month before, when Kaja arrived, and Aura's uniform had been upgraded for one with long sleeves and thick tights. She had felt a bit warmer when Jadelyn walked over, but now that was gone. Still, Aura felt touched by the fact that the new girl had gone out of her way to greet her first.

Why?

Aura happened to look up, and suddenly Jadelyn glanced her way, and their eyes met. Aura was startled, but then Jadelyn smiled briefly at her. By the time Aura remembered to smile back, Jadelyn was looking away.

Yet Aura sensed that the new girl knew how she felt. How *did* she feel, anyway?

Warmer again. And less lonely. What was happening to her?

Jadelyn found herself glancing in Aura's direction quite a bit during the classes that day, especially as she had happened to be seated next to the red-eyed girl herself. Apparently no one usually wanted to sit there, but Jadelyn didn't care, and besides the solitary girl intrigued her. However, Jadelyn didn't really get a chance to talk to her, because as soon as every break began,

Aura got up and walked across the room to the giant window, pressing her face against the glass and watching the snow fall until it was time for the next class. And every time, before Jadelyn could go and join her, she was hooked into a conversation with one or more of the other girls.

The same thing happened at lunch, but Jadelyn was patient. She knew it would only be a matter of time before her popularity as a "new girl" evaporated. Jadelyn had attended many schools before.

However, she was still not expecting one of the popular girls to invite her to sit at her group's table, opposite the leader girl herself. Still less was she expecting the girl to strike up a conversation with her and with her alone, though Jadelyn couldn't help but notice that the other girls didn't seem to realize they were being ignored, they just listened avidly to their leader talking to the new girl. Which was rather strange on its own, even if their leader wasn't the purple-eyed, black-haired girl whose name was Kaja.

"Where do you live?" Kaja's questions came fast and hard, and she leaned across the table, eating while she watched Jadelyn closely out of slightly glimmering purple eyes.

Jadelyn gave her new address, and Kaja fairly beamed at her. "Good, I live near you! We can walk home together."

"I hear you've only lived here a month?" Jadelyn questioned in turn, and Kaja nodded.

"Yes. I used to live further south, but it didn't snow down there," Kaja clarified, then left her answer there, as if it was self-explanatory, though somewhat confusing. "How about you, where are you from?"

"North." Jadelyn grinned. "My parents are glad to move. But it's for my dad's job."

"Sounds interesting," Kaja nodded, and for an instant Jadelyn got the uncomfortable feeling that she was analyzing her. "You have a large family?"

"Well, not as large as some I know," Jadelyn laughed, now completely at ease. "I have a little brother and a sister. But I'm the eldest."

"I had two siblings," Kaja replied slowly, and Jadelyn sensed that Kaja didn't want further inquiry in the subject. "How do you like it at school so far?"

"I think I'm going to love it," Jadelyn returned slowly. As Kaja didn't take up another topic immediately, Jadelyn brought up one of her own. She gestured towards Aura and her lonely table. "Does anyone know her?"

Kaja didn't answer right away, and one of the other girls spoke up for the first time. "Aura? She's a suspect in a murder case," they told Jadelyn eagerly. "Her own foster parents. You don't want to hang out with her."

Suddenly Jadelyn's mind blanked out. "A suspect in a murder case? But… But…"

"It's true," Kaja supplied quietly, and Jadelyn fancied she saw her purple eyes glimmering faintly. "To be honest, she has an alibi for the time when her stepfather was discovered murdered. But not for her foster mother, and it's common knowledge that she hated them both. I hear they hated her as well."

"Yes, and there are rumors that she killed her own real parents as well!" another girl broke in, with a horrified glance towards the loner girl. "As far as I know there is no proof…and I don't know the details, but… Look at her face. Doesn't she look like the killer type to you?"

Even as Jadelyn glanced back in Aura's direction, she could feel the overwhelming atmosphere of hate towards Aura, and it shocked her. Aura's head was downcast, but Jadelyn could still remember the hauntingly sad look in her red eyes.

"Maybe," she returned softly. "So there is no proof? Where is she staying now?"

"Actually, I hear she's living nearby us at the moment," Kaja answered darkly. "But she leaves for school early and goes home late. We won't have any danger of running into her."

Kaja was right, Jadelyn discovered that afternoon when Kaja and her walked to their block together. Aura was nowhere in sight when they left, presumably in some room of the school working on schoolwork, Kaja informed Jadelyn. She soon struck up a friendly conversation with the new girl, and eventually brought up the topic of an ancient legend they had been studying in literature class that afternoon.

"What did you think of it?" she asked Jadelyn quietly.

Jadelyn had been hearing various versions of the story about light, darkness, and creation since as early as she could remember.

"It was okay," she told Kaja vaguely. "What, do you like it?"

"It intrigues me," Kaja replied simply.

"Why?" Jadelyn glanced towards her new friend, suddenly feeling interested as well.

Kaja moved her hands as she tried to explain. "The light, and the darkness… I mean the greater ones, the second ones created. And how the light nearly lost to the darkness, and when it did the world ended." Kaja shrugged. "I think the legend could be changed. It's too simple, and boring."

"Changed how?" Jadelyn wondered.

"Well, the greater darkness should've realized that if it only made the gray grow darker, it would end the world," Kaja explained slowly.

"So you would rather have the greater darkness attack the greater light directly?" Jadelyn laughed. "Good luck with that."

"Oh, no." Suddenly Kaja smiled. "What if the greater darkness merely made it darker, almost black, around just the greater light? What if the light itself dimmed?"

"Dimmed?" Jadelyn frowned. "What do you mean?"

"I mean, what if it lost some of its brightness. The legend also calls the light, life, and hope, doesn't it?" Kaja returned. "What if the light itself lost hope? Then wouldn't the entire world become dark?"

"But that would just end the entire world," Jadelyn pointed out. "In any scenario, that's what happens if the light is completely overwhelmed by the darkness."

"Yes, but it would definitely end it quicker than the method in the legend," Kaja shrugged. "It wouldn't take tens and hundreds of millennia. It would be a lot faster, don't you think?"

"Maybe," Jadelyn admitted almost grudgingly. "Why do you want the world to end faster, though?"

Kaja merely shrugged and walked faster, but Jadelyn's imagination was already sparked.

"If I wrote the legend, I would have there be little lights in the gray, not bright and unfaltering like the greater light is supposed to be, but less dark than the rest of the gray," Jadelyn suggested. "I would have one of them realize what was going on, and at the moment when hope itself was ready to despair, I would have that smaller light give the greater light a spark. And relight it."

"What if the attempt put out the little light itself?" Kaja murmured thoughtfully.

Jadelyn shrugged. "I don't think it would care—do you? Surely it would consider it a just price to save the entire universe from destruction."

"I see." Kaja was walking with her eyes half-closed, but suddenly she stopped, and opened them, glancing at Jadelyn.

"Isn't this your stop?"

A few minutes later, having said her goodbyes and see-you-tomorrows, Jadelyn skipped up the front steps to her family's small home. She didn't look for the key; she knew her family would be home, especially as the primary and middle schools let out earlier than the high school. Jadelyn threw the door open, then turned to wave a final farewell to Kaja before stepping inside the door and closing it behind her.

"Mom, Dad, I'm home!" she called out, heading straight to the living room and swinging her backpack off her back as she went.

At the doorway to the living room, her seven-year-old sister Stacie cannoned into her. Jadelyn just managed to grab the doorpost before she completely fell over.

"Stacie!" she gasped. "What are you doing?"

"Welcome home!" Stacie grabbed her older sister's hand obliviously and pulled her through the living room into the kitchen, where their mother was starting to prepare the dinner. She glanced up briefly as Jadelyn came in.

"Shoes and backpack to your room. Better change out of that uniform as well," her mother added as an afterthought. "Then come back here and help me, will you?"

"Sure thing," Jadelyn replied cheerfully, twisting around until Stacie got dizzy and let go of her. Then Jadelyn made a wild dash for the girls' room, with Stacie chasing after her.

"Jade!" she yowled, until Jadelyn slammed the door, and locked it, almost in her face. "Hey!"

"I'm getting changed!" Jadelyn shouted through the door, afraid for a moment that her sister's vigorous turning of the knob would somehow unlock the faulty old barrier. But finally Stacie gave up and left, probably because the middle sibling, a twelve-year-old brother named Tevin, came by just then wanting Stacie to play with him.

Their voices faded into silence as Jadelyn changed into a casual pink T-shirt and a long, navy-striped skirt and exchanged her stiff, uncomfortable school shoes for a pair of thick, warm socks. It was snowing outside, but Jadelyn almost left her room before she decided to pull on a blue sweater as well.

She met her mother in the kitchen, happy to discover that Tevin and Stacie had gone outside to play. "What can I help with?" Jadelyn asked cheerfully. She liked cooking, and besides it was definitely better than homework.

"Stir the soup, please," her mother directed her. Sliding a pan of homemade rolls into the oven, she wiped her warm hands on her apron, and turned to face Jadelyn briefly. "How was school?"

"I think I'm going to like it," Jadelyn answered, smiling evasively.

"Good." Jadelyn's mother picked up a couple of apples from the counter, chose a cutting board and a knife, and started coring and slicing the fruits. "I'm glad you are finally getting to go to a city school. That's how I was raised."

"Did you like it?" Jadelyn wondered, taking a momentary break from stirring the steaming soup to blow on her somewhat steamed hands.

"Heh! Well enough." Her mother didn't sound too sure about it, Jadelyn thought amusedly. "Make any friends yet?"

"Yeah… The girls seem okay." Jadelyn shrugged. She still wasn't feeling quite comfortable with the hatred-charged school atmosphere, but she expected she was just making too much of it. Personally, she liked Aura. And a few of the other girls as well. And she guessed she liked Kaja. Jadelyn had never been friends with any of the super popular girls at her old school, and she wasn't sure she was going to like it here. But she would find out, wouldn't she?

"Guess you'll find out," her mother said, and Jadelyn started, wondering for just a brief moment whether her mother could read her mind. But of course not. "How much homework do you have?"

"Umm, well, I'm a transfer student, so not too much today, I think," Jadelyn answered, meanwhile wondering exactly how much homework she really *did* have.

"Good, then maybe you can do some shopping for me after dinner," her mother decided happily, but then she glanced at the clock. "What, almost six already? When does your father get home from work?" she muttered to herself. "Hey, Jadelyn, I think that's ready. Just take it off the burner."

Jadelyn did so, turning off the burner as well. Besides loving cooking, she was also quite good at it, though her favorite and specialty was baking. She dreamed of running a bakery shop when she grew older.

"Should I go call the kids in?" she wondered, but her mother shook her head.

"No, wait till your father comes home. Set the table, though, will you?"

At dinner, eventually the conversation was changed to what the children had learnt at school that day, and Stacie was quick to bring up the ancient folktale legend her class had been studying.

"We studied the old musty thing last year at our old school, too," she proclaimed disgustedly. "Why does it seem so important?"

"That's because the Festival of Light is coming up," her father informed her, smiling at his wife. "You know what that is, don't you?"

Stacie was quick to assert her knowledge. "Of course I do, Dad! It's the day everyone is supposed to be kind to each other. And the weatherman picks a day the sun is supposed to come out, so everyone will naturally be cheerful."

Jadelyn actually almost choked on her food. "I'd like to see the sun come out here! It's done nothing but snow and storm the entire time."

"We've only been here a few days," her father reminded her gently, and Jadelyn shrugged. But it was snowing even then.

"We were learning about the Festival origins," Tevin put in pensively. "It comes from that legend, Stacie. Because there's a tradition that the weather matches how gray or how bright the world is, and when people are happy and hopeful together, the sun comes out."

"I already knew that," Stacie told him indignantly. "And I learned something new today, too. My teacher said that if the brighter light in the legend is alive and in the world, the weather in its area matches how brightly its light is shining."

Jadelyn nodded thoughtfully. "I remember learning that… Oh, wow," she interrupted herself suddenly, and stopped eating.

Her parents glanced at her curiously. "What's wrong?" her mother inquired.

"I wouldn't get into trouble if I wrote another version of the legend, would I?" Jadelyn asked quickly, her blue eyes filled with excitement. "One where the brighter light ended up winning?"

"Well, I wouldn't think so," her father smiled. "It's not like the legends are important in themselves, anyway. Just don't be too casual about it, since our entire culture is based on the one about light and darkness."

"I won't," she assured him eagerly, gulping down the rest of her plate's contents, which wasn't much. She glanced up expectantly. "May I please be excused?"

That evening, as soon as she had finished her homework, which luckily didn't take her too long, Jadelyn retreated to her bunk bed armed with paper and a pen. Stacie had already fallen asleep, and in the first hour or two of the next morning, Jadelyn penned away at her personal version of the Legend of Creation, pausing every few minutes to stop and choose her next words. She was determined to make this the best thing she had ever written, even if it would be short.

But towards the end of her story she kept getting sleepier, and sleepier, and eventually shoved the paper and pen aside, since she couldn't concentrate anymore and she was afraid she would make a mistake. She was dimly annoyed that thoughts of Kaja and Aura kept coming into her head. In her last thoughts awake, she seemed to see them locked in an eternal supernatural conflict. Or maybe that was her dream. Because when she woke up, it was because she'd had a nightmare about Kaja chasing her with a knife.

Very pleasant, she thought to herself grimly as she rubbed her eyes and glanced out the window. She sighed. It wasn't snowing, but the entire sky was still a dark, depressing gray. Or was that just because it was early on a winter morning?

Suddenly she heard the city bells chiming seven o'clock, and she slowly got out of bed, climbing down drowsily from her bunk. Stacie was waking up now as well, and the two got dressed into their uniforms quickly. The air was freezing. Stacie's uniform was simpler, and she finished quicker, pulling on her backpack and flipping the day on her mini-calendar before running out the door. Jadelyn buttoned her knee-high black boots slowly, glancing across the room at her sister's calendar as she did so. In the corner of the colorful picture that stated the date, Stacie had scribbled a note: *12 days until the Festival!*

Only twelve days left, Jadelyn thought to herself, smiling as she stood up and grabbed her blazer, sliding it on. When that was done she only had to grab her backpack, put that on, and go out the door herself. Some minutes later she was on her way to school, having already split up with her siblings.

Her mother had given her a hot cream-filled bagel to eat on the way, and Jadelyn was glad to eat it. She hurried before the breakfast got cold or maybe even froze; she could see her breath in the air. But the food warmed her hands momentarily.

Suddenly she remembered her story she'd been writing when she fell asleep, and smiled helplessly. She couldn't wait to get back home and finish it.

Jadelyn hurried on along her route, unaware that above her, the dark, heavy clouds parted for a moment, and the rare sunlight shone through.

Five

So the two were placed in the world, Light and Darkness. But even then the world was not all the same gray. There were spots of darker gray, where people lost hope, where they despaired. And then spots of lighter gray, where they were cheerful and did their best to make their surroundings cheerful as well. So, when the brighter Light and the darker Darkness were created, no one else knew who they were, and neither did they themselves know, at least at first.

The greater Darkness discovered its identity first. It had been born, and lived, but since it was Death itself, it was not alive. But the greater Darkness, once it found that out, was not satisfied with its fate. It did not immediately seek to destroy the Light, but instead took up a disguise. It strove to appear to be the greater Light—or at least one of the brighter gray lights. And so the world was deceived, and the brighter Light, which was the world's Life, was unaware of its own existence.

Festival of Darkness

THE DAY BEFORE the Festival of Light, it was dark and gloomy as always. But a certain, brown-haired, blue-eyed girl of sixteen walked quickly and hurriedly along her way to school. It was obvious from the way she kept glancing around that she was expecting to meet up with someone somewhere on her way, but equally obvious that she was doubtful she had left at the right time. However, suddenly Jadelyn spotted two figures up ahead, both of which she recognized, and she stopped short for a moment before shrugging her shoulders and continuing alone.

The two figures were Aura and Eva. Eva had more or less unofficially renounced her friendship with Aura shortly after her foster parents had been murdered, but now it looked to Jadelyn like the two were making up. She'd wanted to speak to Aura, but since Eva was already doing that, Jadelyn decided to leave them alone. She could probably get a chance to talk with Aura later.

Meanwhile, Eva and Aura were indeed making up. In the past few days, tension between the main group of high school students and Aura had reached a breaking point, and as Eva told Aura, she hadn't wanted to betray her friend in the first place. Aura just listened, and gradually managed a small smile.

"So why did you?" she asked finally, and Eva shrugged helplessly.

"I guess I just wanted to go with the crowd, Aura. But they're going too far.

They have no right to hate you, and besides, I know you wouldn't murder anybody!" Eva told her emphatically. "So, you and I, we can defy them together! Are we friends again?"

Aura hesitated only a moment before holding out her hand simply. "We've always been friends, Eva. I just…"

"What is it?" Eva asked her quietly, taking her friend's hand.

"Can we promise never to hurt each other?" Aura whispered, and then drew in a breath of cold air sharply. "I mean, I know I'm a pathetic friend and all that, but I… I just…"

"Never again," Eva told her warmly. "I won't hurt you ever again. I promise."

Aura's red eyes were dim with tears. "Thanks," she managed to say stiffly. "I won't either."

"You never hurt me," Eva laughed. "You don't have it in you to hurt anyone. That's how I'm sure you couldn't have murdered them."

"But sometimes I feel so angry." Aura clenched her fists, and they kept walking. "At everyone. At myself. I'm afraid it'll come out."

Eva squeezed her hand, and the fist dissolved. "Sometimes it's okay to be angry, and it's always okay to be sad. You can just never give up hope. Whether for yourself or for someone else."

"There is one thing I've completely given up hope in," Aura admitted, cheering up somewhat. "Darkness."

"Haha, you're funny," Eva giggled. "Speaking of which, have you got plans for the Festival of Light tomorrow?"

"Not really. I mean, not that I know of. My foster parents haven't spoken about it; I think they have work," Aura told her, and shrugged carelessly.

"Poor folks," Eva murmured sympathetically. "My family is taking a trip to the capital, but I'm sure I can get out of that if you want to go walking together after school?" she wondered.

"Don't you want to go to the capital, too?" Aura asked, her eyebrows shooting up.

"Oh, I've been there plenty of times," Eva shrugged carelessly. "I just feel like spending the day with you."

"That's sweet of you, but—"

"No buts," Eva interrupted her, grinning. "So, a walk? Yes or no? Just us two?"

"Sounds good to me," Aura murmured, her red eyes alight with happiness. "You know what, this is like the old days, Eva."

"Isn't it?" Eva smiled, and laughed. "And I'm going to make you late, as usual, unless we hurry!"

That day at school was a peaceful one, to all appearances. Jadelyn kept waiting for a chance to talk to Aura, but even though her information was somewhat urgent she eventually decided against telling her that day.

Aura seemed happy to be reunited with Eva, who was true to her word about not hurting Aura again. She talked to her in every five-minute break and during the lunch break as well, despite the only-too-obvious glares from the other girls.

That night, Jadelyn went home satisfied. She herself had thought of cheering up the lonesome red-eyed girl as her special Festival of Light task—it was her family's tradition for each of them to choose a certain person who was down and depressed, and invite them to go somewhere fun with them—but if Eva was going to be taking Aura along with her, Jadelyn could find someone else.

The morning of the Festival of Light dawned a more beautiful and sunny day than any that city had seen for a long, long time, and Jadelyn was pleasantly surprised, as was her "Festival-Friend" she'd picked up, a red-haired ninth-grader named Chanelle, with a noticeable lisp that made her somewhat unpopular among her classmates. They took a bus to the nearby countryside area where there was going to be an actual Light Festival that evening.

"Sit in the back of the bus and no one can sit behind you," Jadelyn grinned as she sat down in the back, and the younger girl laughed.

Jadelyn had no problems with keeping a conversation going, and so the half-hour's drive passed in pleasant small talk with Chanelle. When they arrived, it was early afternoon; and since the sun set early in the winter, lanterns were already being hung out on strings between the trees surrounding the clearing. Chanelle, who by now was being quite social, happily informed Jadelyn that the place was a traditional Festival of Light gathering place, called Kanjest Woods.

"It means 'Light Dance' in one of the older Northern languages," she explained. "My family used to come here every year. The stars always shine brighter on the night of the Festival of Light, did you know that?"

"That's what everyone always says," Jadelyn agreed, glancing up at the quickly darkening sky thoughtfully. "How long until it gets dark, do you think?"

"Oh, half an hour or so," Chanelle estimated. She sniffed the air, smiling. "They've started cooking dinner. Want to grab some?"

Fifteen minutes later found the two girls walking around the edges of the clearing, eating their dinner and talking together about how cold it was and whether winter was the best season or not.

Suddenly a voice interjected a comment from above them, and both girls stopped short and stared up into the branches of a tree. The light was getting dimmer every minute, but they could just make out the outline of a young man around eighteen years old, working with the lantern strings.

"Winter is good when it isn't stormy," he had said. Now he smiled upon seeing the girls' surprise. "Sorry, did I interrupt you? Oh, wait, dinner is ready already?"

"Yeah," Jadelyn answered both questions in one shot, having gotten over her brief surprise by now. The man slid down athletically from the tree, and now the girls could see him clearly. Jadelyn liked him on sight. He had rather longish and curly dark brown hair, and his eyes were a bright, almost shining green. Something about him seemed familiar, but Jadelyn couldn't tell what it was.

"My name's Niran," he introduced himself cheerfully, blowing on his hands. "Man, it's cold alright. Mind if I walk with you?"

"Sure," Chanelle shrugged carelessly. "I'm Chanelle."

"Jadelyn, but everyone calls me Jade," Jadelyn added in turn.

The man glanced sharply at her. "You've got an accent. North?"

"Yeah, sort of," Jadelyn laughed. "But you don't sound like you're from around here, either," she observed.

Niran shrugged. "I'm not. I'm really just here at Kanjest to help out with the festival." Noting their uniforms, he grinned. "You go to the high school here?"

"You seem to know a lot about this area," Jadelyn returned evasively. Niran didn't seem to mind.

"What's the city like?" he wondered as they neared the bonfires. The girls had to hurry to keep up with him.

"It's pretty okay—ooo!" Chanelle broke off as suddenly a cold wind, stronger and colder than any before that winter, nearly blew them off their feet. Suddenly the whole sky seemed darker, and Jadelyn began shivering. The three stopped walking.

Niran glanced up as the sky clouded over. "And tonight was supposed to be clear," he muttered, tucking his bare hands inside his sleeves. "Well, that was fast. And look, the fires have gone out."

Chanelle was shivering even harder than Jadelyn. "Jade, let's go back to the city," she stammered. Jadelyn took her hand.

Niran walked along with them, rubbing his hands together frantically. "And I'll have to walk two hours to get back to the college campus!" he sighed.

"Why don't you just catch the bus to the city?" Jadelyn wondered, feeling somewhat sorry for him. "There's no school tomorrow, so you can probably get back to your college tomorrow, wherever it is."

Suddenly Niran smiled. "I actually really like that idea," he admitted. "You two don't mind, do you?"

"'Course not," Chanelle shrugged.

"You two keep going, then—the bus stop is that way—I'm going to grab some leftover dinner and then I'll catch up with you," Niran promised. Throwing the girls a casual salute, he ran off, leaving them to press on alone.

"Is this a good idea, Jade?" Chanelle asked doubtfully.

Jadelyn was trying to remember whom Niran reminded her of. "He seems alright to me," she admitted absently, throwing her head back to look at the sky. "Well, it's dark enough to be midnight, but I don't see any stars, do you?"

"How odd," Chanelle breathed, following her older friend's example. "I don't see any, either. This is the first Festival of Light I haven't seen the stars."

"Festival of Darkness, more like," Jadelyn murmured; but then she remembered the part of the legend where when the brighter Light grew dim, so did the sky.

Jadelyn shuddered. "Chanelle, let's hurry," she urged.

"Yeah," Chanelle agreed simply. "I think it's going to storm."

Just as they were nearing the bus stop, which was the center of the small town near the Kanjest Woods, Niran caught up with them.

"Oh, there you are," he grinned. "Bus arrives in two minutes, right?"

The ride home was an enjoyable one, what with Niran's telling the two girls funny stories of his life at college, but when they arrived in the city and everyone said goodbye, Jadelyn found the darkness and cold depressing. As she rushed home, she felt so cold she was afraid she would freeze. If she looked at the porch roofs of houses she passed she could see icicles.

Everyone complained about the weather that night, and Jadelyn was glad to eventually tumble into bed and try to be warm again. She didn't know anything of what had happened that afternoon, in the city itself. Not yet.

But it had been about when the weather turned dark, before which it had been at its brightest and warmest. Aura and Eva had been walking together, looking at the shops: a trending high school girl pastime, Eva claimed. Aura had been feeling happier than she had felt in a long time. They were about to go into a restaurant and have supper when the driverless truck came rushing down the street. Eva didn't have a chance, and Aura was only missed by what seemed incredible luck.

Her golden-haired friend hadn't even had time to scream before the truck slammed into her, tearing her hand out of Aura's as it careened wildly down the slope with Eva in front and eventually underneath. When it stopped some meters later, crashing into a lamppost and twisting horribly, Aura ran over, screaming her friend's name.

"Eva!" she cried; and suddenly seemed to see something in the truck driver's seat, something so terrifying that Eva's name turned into a short-lived shriek as Aura tripped on a cobblestone and slammed forward. Gasping for breath, Aura glanced back up at the truck; but the driver's seat was empty again.

It was then that she realized her scraped hands had landed in something wet. And it wasn't all her blood. Not the crimson that was splattered all over the front of the truck, and the lamppost, and the pavement around her.

As if in a dream, Aura saw her friend's hand reaching out from underneath the truck, as if Eva had been trying to reach for Aura's.

Aura screamed for help, tears streaming down her face as she grasped her friend's hand.

Above them, the sky grew dark. And then Aura heard something. Or *thought* she heard something—in a voice she knew, too.

Except the voice was colder than it usually was.

"Do you know yet how I feel?"

Aura gasped and glanced around. Other people were arriving on the scene, people who were asking her what had happened, if she was alright, and everything else imaginable.

Look around as she would, Aura didn't see the person whose voice she had heard, and she tried to dismiss it as her imagination. But whenever she remembered the tone of the voice, or the phantom truck driver, she shuddered.

When the paramedics finally arrived, it didn't take them long to announce that Eva had no chance of survival. One young woman took charge of Aura, wiping off her bloodied hands for her and bundling her up against the sudden cold, trying to find out who she was and where she lived.

Aura was unresponsive. For the first time in her life, she was frozen cold in a dark world of her own, with nothing but black horror around her, and the paramedic took one look at her dim red eyes and decided she was in deep shock.

Aura didn't hear that, and neither did she notice when a man who'd been following her and Eva emerged from the crowd, telling the paramedics that the girl's first name was Aura and that he could guide the paramedics to her home.

When questioned as to his identity, he quietly informed the paramedic leader that he was a detective investigating a murder case in which Aura was a suspect.

"But," he added, "I don't think it could have been her. But let's get her home."

And so they did, and explained the situation to her foster parents, who took charge of Aura in turn. Her foster mother, looking concerned, put Aura to bed, leaving a cup of hot chocolate on her nightstand; but, suddenly, Aura seemed to wake up somewhat, and put her hand on her foster mother's arm just as the woman was turning to leave.

"Eva is dead, isn't she?" Her face, and her dull red eyes, were surprisingly blank and emotionless.

Her foster mother didn't really want to tell her, but she realized that after her first moment of hesitation Aura would know the truth, if she didn't already.

"Yes," she told her finally, and simply. "Do you want anything?"

Aura shook her head mutely, and turned towards the window; her foster mother left the room, closing the door softly.

In the room behind her, Aura stared out at the forming blizzard and wept. And the sky wept with her.

"Eva," she whispered. "You said you wouldn't hurt me anymore."

Seven

IV

Once its position was solidified, the greater Darkness set about dimming the brighter Light. As the Light didn't know it was the Light, it soon grew dim, overwhelmed by the intensity of the hateful darkness around it. And as the Light dimmed, so did the world's gray grow darker. It would not be long until the brighter Light died out completely, and then surely the darker Darkness would overtake and envelope the world in its everlasting, frozen night.

But there was one of the spots of lighter gray, that gradually came to realize that that one, dying, despairing Light was actually the greater Light. That spot of gray realized that to save the world it would have to somehow make the greater Light shine again, and before it was too late. For when that greater Light went completely out, it would be the End of the World.

Eight

The Unfinished Legend

J ADELYN WAS WAITING. It was the Monday after the Festival of Light that had ended in complete darkness, and after the tragic accident in the streets of Coloni. Jadelyn had heard about the incident and had gone to the funeral on Saturday, but she hadn't seen Aura there, and she wondered if Aura would be coming to school.

Now, as she sat waiting on the steps, sitting against the wall and trying to ignore the fierce outside cold, her numb fingers were wrapped around a small package.

Jadelyn sighed. It wasn't like she had good news for Aura, anyway. What Jadelyn had wanted to tell her on Thursday, was that Jadelyn's family was moving away, back to where they had come from. Jadelyn might have felt glad if she hadn't realized she was leaving someone like Aura behind.

At least she had something to give her.

She glanced up as she heard approaching footsteps, and smiled. It was Aura.

Swiftly Jadelyn stood up, going to meet the newcomer.

Aura's red eyes were downcast, and her shoulders drooping, but when she realized someone was standing in front of her she stopped, looked up, and shook the snow off her shoulders.

"Hi," Jadelyn told her quietly. Aura brushed by her, heading for the bench where she usually sat. Nonplussed, Jadelyn followed her.

"I wanted to give you something," she continued, ignoring the fact that she was seemingly being ignored. She held out the package. "We're moving back next week, and I…I probably won't be back for a while. So I wanted to give you this." Jadelyn swallowed.

Unexpectedly, Aura looked up and asked an even more unexpected question. "Jade? Do you believe in ghosts?"

"What?" Jadelyn asked, startled at the haunting look in Aura's eyes.

"Never mind… Oh, Jadelyn, that's so nice of you. What is it?" Aura murmured, having finally noticed the package Jadelyn was holding out to her.

Jadelyn placed it in the girl's lap. "Nothing much," she admitted, blushing as Aura carefully unwrapped the package—almost too carefully.

It was a small notebook. The first few pages were covered in Jadelyn's neat handwriting, but the rest were empty.

Aura scanned the first few lines, then stopped and glanced up at Jadelyn. "This is the legend of Light and Darkness," she interpreted, confused.

Jadelyn nodded energetically. "It is, but I started rewriting it." She giggled self-consciously, then got serious again. "I haven't finished. Aura, I want you to finish it."

"Me?" Aura's face was blank. "Why?"

"Because the original is depressing, isn't it? When Darkness overtakes Light and the world ends?" Jadelyn smiled. "Someday, Aura, I hope you'll be happy. Really happy. And then I want you to take this story out and finish it."

Aura shook her head slowly. "You ought to finish it, Jade. It's your story."

"It's yours now," Jade insisted brightly.

Taking a deep breath, she decided to take the plunge. "Hey, Aura, I wanted to say this on Thursday but… I didn't get a chance. I know I'm moving next week, but are we friends?" she asked slowly. "Maybe you're mad at me, but…"

Aura's voice was incredulous. "Mad at you?" she asked, and laughed shortly. "No. That's one of my problems. I can never be mad at anyone."

"That's not a problem, that sounds like a good thing," Jadelyn laughed, unaware that that oddity had cost Aura many insults and taunts in her primary school years. "That's good, then. Oh, and I'm sorry…about Eva," she finished dully.

"Don't say sorry to me," Aura murmured, slowly folding up the papers Jadelyn had given her. "In a way it's my fault. I should have known that being friends with a—a murderer like me—would have gotten her into trouble." She winced. "No, I'm not a murderer, am I?"

"Of course not," Jadelyn snorted, though she was slightly disturbed.

Suddenly Aura glanced up, her red eyes shining brighter than usual—or was that her imagination?

Jadelyn wondered.

"No, Jade, don't do this to yourself. Believe me." Aura spoke quietly—but earnestly. "You don't want to be friends with me."

"I do," Jadelyn insisted indignantly. "Whatever gave you that idea? Or do you not want to be friends with me?"

"No, I just… Jadelyn, please don't. If you are my friend you'll be hurt, too."

Suddenly Jadelyn thought she saw something else in Aura's eyes, besides sadness—a terrible horror.

She started, taking a step back. "Aura, what's wrong? Is there…is there something I don't know?"

"The truck that hit my friend wasn't empty," Aura told Jadelyn later during lunch, her voice low, her eyes downcast. "I saw someone. But was it real, or am I going insane?"

"But the police checked the truck, and no one was there!" Jadelyn protested, startled.

Aura shook her head. "No, I'm sure I saw someone—or something."

She shuddered, and Jadelyn could tell instinctively that her red-eyed friend was telling the truth.

"There is only one word for what I saw, Jade." Aura looked straight at Jadelyn. "A demon."

"Really?" Jadelyn asked doubtfully. "What did it look like?"

Aura closed her eyes, remembering. "It was like something like out of a nightmare. The worst thing is that I recognized it—and the voice."

"It spoke?" Jadelyn's eyebrows shot up. "And you…*recognized* it?"

Aura nodded her head simply. "Yes. 'Do you know yet how I feel?'"

"That's weird," Jadelyn muttered sensibly. She shook off her head. "And what did it look like?"

The other girl shuddered again. "What it really was was darkness. But… Bright, glowing purple eyes. And hair so dark it would have stood out on a dark night. Her clothing was dark as well, but with a strange blue radiance."

Aura shook her head. "I'm sorry. You must think I'm crazy."

"Well…" Jadelyn was at a loss. "But it was…familiar?"

Aura hesitated. "It reminded me of…my…my sister, and…Kaja."

"Kaja?" Jadelyn echoed in disbelief. "You have a sister?"

Suddenly she sensed eyes on her back, and she wheeled around, only to find that no one was watching her—and also to find that her original repugnance towards Kaja had returned in full force. Quickly Jadelyn turned back towards Aura, staring hard at her face.

"Well, I *had* a sister," Aura told her slowly. "A twin. But she died as a baby."

"Well, then how did you—"

"I don't know!" Aura broke in suddenly. She leaned across the table towards Jadelyn. "All I know, Jade, is that I keep seeing that face since a month and a half ago. Which is when—"

"When Kaja came to this city," Jadelyn supplied, and a chill ran up and down her spine.

Aura hesitated only a moment before nodding. "Yes. Do you ever feel weird around her, or is it just me?"

Jadelyn did, but she didn't want to admit there was anything ethereal going on. "Say, a month and a half ago is when your former foster parents were murdered, isn't it?" she asked her thoughtfully.

"It is," Aura admitted, glancing down at the table before back at Jadelyn.

"Well, you were probably traumatized, right?" Jadelyn suggested. "So you could be imagining you're seeing and hearing things. Are you sleeping well?"

Aura's red eyes narrowed. "I have nightmares every night," she informed Jadelyn. "Always have. But I haven't always seen my sister everywhere."

"Listen, Aura, I think you need a little more light in your life," Jadelyn told her firmly. "Don't you have any other friends?"

Aura hesitated only a moment before shaking her head.

"Then come with me after classes," Jadelyn decided. She smiled as she downed the rest of her cup of water. "I want you to meet someone."

The bell rang then, and the girls filed uniformly out of the lunch room, back to their respective classrooms, and the day's schoolwork resumed. As they left, a hooded figure slipped out of the shadows by the table Jadelyn and Aura had sat at, and headed for the school exit.

As he left, the rare winter sunlight fell on his face, revealing dark brown hair and bright green eyes, that reflected the light as he quickly glanced around him before descending the steps and walking hurriedly across the schoolyard towards the gate and the street.

After school, Aura in tow, Jadelyn started walking around the juniors' building and towards that of the ninth graders.

"I can't stay too long or my foster parents will be worried," Aura told Jadelyn conscientiously.

"It'll be alright," Jadelyn assured her brightly. "This will only take a minute."

As they approached the building, Jadelyn waved to a red-haired girl that was walking down the path, alone. "Hoy! Chanelle!"

The girl turned, seeing them for the first time. She stopped in her tracks. "Jade!"

Quickly Jadelyn led Aura over, and promptly introduced the two. "Hey, Chanelle! I'd like you to meet my friend, Aura. Aura, this is Chanelle."

Upon hearing Aura's name, Chanelle's freckled face got slightly whiter, and she glanced doubtfully at Jadelyn. "Your friend…?"

"Right," Jadelyn affirmed energetically. "The girl suspected for murder. Sound familiar?"

"I…" Chanelle's voice trailed off, and even if she didn't intend to let it, Aura's face fell slightly.

Jadelyn laughed. "It's fine, you two. Chanelle, Aura is one of the gentlest girls alive, okay? Do you remember what I told you on Thursday?"

"Yeah. You're moving away next week," Chanelle nodded, somewhat unenthusiastically.

"Exactly, which is why I want you two to be friends." Jadelyn grinned at them, taking Aura's hand first, and then Chanelle's, and putting the two's hands together. "You're both loners. And so when I'm gone, I want you to talk to each other and be each other's friend. Alright?" she asked cheerfully.

Aura glanced at Chanelle. Their eyes locked.

"Alright," they said together. And then they smiled, and Jadelyn smiled with them.

About half an hour later, Aura arrived at the apartment that had been her home for the past few weeks, since she had been taken in by new foster parents. Though obviously they were obligated to provide for her, they had been extremely busy at work as of late, and Aura's presence was mostly ignored, a circumstance which suited her habits fine. But today was different. When she walked in the door, she could smell dinner already cooking.

Aura's heart leapt, and she stopped short, her eyes suddenly misting over. She wiped her face with her sleeve, abashed. Why was she letting so many things get to her lately?

But for an instant she had remembered one of those rare happy days in her childhood, one when her old foster father had come home early from work and made dinner, a wonderful, scrumptious dinner, for Aura's seventh birthday.

"I'm home!" she called out, her voice gay and cheerful for the moment before it faltered. There was no immediate answer, but Aura hadn't really expected one, and she headed down the hall towards her bedroom to start homework.

Suddenly her foster mother called her name. "Aura, would you come in here, please? Once you're done changing?"

"Okay!" Aura had never changed faster in her life.

Within sixty seconds, she was in the kitchen, rolling up the sleeves of her jacket as she saw her foster mother was definitely going to need her help with the cooking. Aura was startled when the woman turned and smiled at her as she entered the room.

"I've quit my job," she announced unexpectedly, and then began struggling under the weight of a large pan of fried rice.

Aura leapt for it, grabbing the other handle just in time. Helping her foster mother steady the dish, she asked her, "Why?"

"Your foster father and I talked it over," her foster mother explained as they got the pan onto the table. "Aura, do you know why we asked you if you wanted to come live with us?"

Aura merely shrugged. She had figured the orphanage had been looking for somewhere Aura could stay, just to get her off their hands. But apparently not.

"We have always wanted children," her foster mother went on quietly, "but it was not meant to be. And then we heard you needed a place to stay."

Well, I guess the orphanage was asking around after all, Aura thought humorlessly to herself.

"So we asked you, and you said yes," her foster mother continued. "But, you see, my husband and I didn't realize that if we were going to adopt we would have to change our lifestyle. It's not that we didn't want you—it's that we have never had experience with children—young adults before," she corrected herself, smiling. "But, Aura, I hope we haven't hurt you."

"Of course not," Aura murmured, wondering where this was going.

"I'm afraid we were neglecting you, though," her foster mother frowned. "But I realized…when your friend was hit by that truck… We need to be with you more, and spend more time with you. I just hope it isn't too late."

She paused. "I did tell you I'm sorry about your friend, right?"

"Yes," Aura nodded simply. Her foster mother had told her that at least half a dozen times over the weekend, but somehow this time Aura realized she really meant it.

"Then I hope you'll forgive me, and your foster father, when he comes home from work," the woman told her adopted daughter, smiling hopefully.

Suddenly Aura felt her eyes brimming with tears.

"There's nothing to forgive," she managed to reply. "Thank you for letting me be a part of your family."

That night, Aura sat on her bed and began to complete her homework. It was slow going, as she couldn't stop thinking about the conversation she and her new parents had had over the dinner table. Her life had definitely changed for the better—and so had the weather, she couldn't help but notice.

If she glanced out the window she could see the stars shining brightly in the winter night sky.

She was just pulling out her English folder when a folded paper fell out of it, into her lap. She unfolded it carefully. No, it was two papers. The story Jadelyn had given her to finish.

Aura read it completely for the first time, then refolded it, smiling to herself. She had homework still to finish, and besides she didn't know what she would write for the story's ending, not yet at least. She was happy tonight, but there would be other nights, she was sure.

She would wait to finish the legend.

Nine

$\mathcal{V}$

Gradually other brighter gray spots gathered around the brighter Light as well, and the Light itself grew brighter. It seemed that the greater Darkness's attempt had failed, and the world would be saved. For a time, it seemed as if the Darkness, and even the gray, would be completely overwhelmed. For when the Light became aware of its power and shone to its full brightness, that would be the end of the Darkness. For Light is stronger than Darkness, Hope is stronger than Despair, and Life stronger than Death.

But the greater Darkness was aware of the situation. What the lighter gray spots did not realize was that everything was going according to Darkness's plan. If there were lighter gray spots around the brighter Light, and then those spots were blotted out, the Light would only get darker, and then eventually be obliterated. And it would be no trouble at all for the lighter gray spots to be put out.

Ten

The Sun Shines

THE NEXT MONDAY, Jadelyn met with Chanelle and Aura after school—for the last time.

"I'm going to miss you both," she told them, hugging each of them once and then again. "But we'll meet again someday, won't we?"

"We definitely will," Chanelle returned brightly. "I'm sorry, you two. I really have to go now."

"See you soon, Chanelle," Jadelyn and Aura told their friend together, and after a cheery wave, Chanelle set off on her way home.

Aura glanced at Jadelyn. "I should be heading home as well," she admitted quietly.

Jadelyn threw her arm around her somewhat older friend's shoulders. "Let's walk together," she grinned, and Aura nodded.

For the first few minutes they walked together in silence, then Jadelyn happened to glance up at the sky.

"Isn't the weather beautiful?" she asked dreamily. "Spring has got to be on the way."

"No spring can be better than last week," Aura told her emphatically, and Jadelyn laughed self-consciously.

"Really, Aura, there is light and happiness everywhere you look if you know what to look for," she grinned.

"I'm glad we were friends," Aura whispered, and Jadelyn glanced at her.

"Huh?"

"I'm glad we were friends. Even if you have to leave."

"We're *still* friends, Aura," Jadelyn reminded her. "We always will be."

"Thanks," Aura murmured, her eyes alight. "You'll write to me, right?"

"Of course!" Jadelyn told her, incredulous that such a thing wasn't obvious. "And you have to write back, too. And you have to finish my story!"

"I will," Aura promised brightly. "I'll finish it soon, and then I'll send you a copy."

"Better make it a happy ending, and then I'll publish it for you," Jadelyn offered. Aura scoffed and threw a punch into the air.

"You publish it and I'll—" she began, then stopped. "Well, you wrote half of it anyway."

"Half!" Jadelyn snorted. "I definitely wrote more than half."

They continued their friendly bantering for a couple of minutes, and then Aura stopped suddenly, in front of a rather gray-looking apartment building.

"Well, this is my stop." She sighed.

Jadelyn's eyes sparkled. "Would it be okay if I came in for a few minutes?"

Aura was only too happy to introduce her friend to her foster parents, who were sad that Jadelyn had to leave but hoped she had enjoyed her experience in Coloni, and thanked her for coming to visit. They would have asked her to stay for dinner, but Jadelyn admitted that she would have to hurry home to get back in time for the family's tight moving schedule.

"Well, goodbye," Aura told her finally.

Jadelyn looked hard at her for a moment, then threw her arms around her friend and pressed something into her hand.

"'Bye," she murmured, and then left, skipping down the apartment building steps as was her custom.

Aura stood by her bedroom window, watching and waiting until she could see Jadelyn walking merrily down the street. As if the brown-haired girl could sense Aura was watching her, she turned suddenly and waved in the direction of the window.

Aura waved back, until Jadelyn was out of sight. Then slowly and reluctantly she started to leave her bedroom—and stopped.

There was a shadow in the hallway, just outside her bedroom door. Not a moving shadow, but one that was just standing there, presumably watching her from around the corner.

Aura's spine tingled. "Hello?" she asked softly, but no one answered.

Face your fears, Aura reminded herself. Bracing, she suddenly ran over to the door, peering up and down the hallway.

She blinked in surprise. No one was there, and the shadow was gone.

Puzzled, Aura rubbed her eyes.

And then she heard that horrible, terrifyingly sarcastic voice. "You can't run from fate. Why do you try, Aura?"

For a moment Aura's heart stopped. Gradually the sensation dissipated, leaving behind an overwhelming feeling of horrified distaste.

That voice. Aura couldn't hate many things, but she *could* hate that voice. It rang in her ears, mockingly reminding her of both her twin sister and—Kaja.

"Aura? Hello, Aura?"

Her foster mother was calling her.

Aura tried to make herself forget the voice and the shadow as she ran to answer the call. "I'm coming!"

A few days later, Aura was doing work in the yard with her foster mother, but the sun eventually began setting, and her foster mother went in to start dinner, as Aura had offered to finish up in the yard alone. Working slowly but steadily, she finished the row of bulbs by the fence, ignoring the city sounds from the street.

Aura smiled as she imagined to herself what the tulips would look like in a couple of weeks when they began to grow.

Carefully she smoothed the loose, cold soil over the last bulb and wiped off her gloves. She was just about to stand up when she heard a voice.

"Excuse me, Miss?"

Glancing up, Aura caught sight of a young man standing just outside the fence. He was wearing a hood, which cast a shadow over his face, so she couldn't really see what he looked like, but he sounded friendly, albeit slightly familiar.

Aura stood up, smiling tentatively. "Yeah?" she asked.

"Do you know a Miss Jadelyn who attends the high school here?" the man asked her. "Eleventh grade, I believe?"

"Actually, she just moved," Aura replied. "Why?"

Her question wasn't immediately answered. "What about a Miss Chanelle? I think she's a ninth-grader?"

"I do know her," Aura admitted. "But I don't know where she lives."

The young man shrugged. "That's fine. Could you please give this to her, then, next time you see her? I was traveling with them almost two weeks ago and one of them dropped this. I'm sorry I didn't get a chance to return it before now—could you tell her that for me, please?"

As he spoke, he reached his hand into his pocket, pulling out a small envelope. He handed it across the fence to Aura, and she could feel something like a hairpin inside it.

Aura was about to tell him she'd do as he requested, but she happened to look up at his face again, and saw that his motion had made his hood move slightly. Her eyes widened immediately.

"Thanks," the young man murmured as he turned to leave.

But suddenly Aura reached out, grasping his arm. The young man looked at her, his eyes narrowing in surprise as he noted Aura's serious, almost desperate expression. "Is something wrong?"

"Sorry," Aura whispered, her voice tight. But she had to ask. "Do you—do you know a certain Madden Eienno?"

"Know him?" The man looked startled, but then he recovered himself. "That's my late father's name. I'm Niran Eienno. Why?"

"What?" Aura demanded incredulously. "He is—*was*—your father? From Canasili? A tall man, with bright green eyes, and—hair like yours?"

Niran merely nodded, being quite confused. "That was him. Why?"

Suddenly letting go of Niran's hand, Aura reached for the gate, throwing it open. "Please come in. My name—my name is Aura Eienno."

When she had explained the same thing to her foster parents, who were at first quite shocked when Aura practically dragged in a stranger a couple of years older than her, her foster father seemed pleasantly surprised, and her foster mother delighted. But Aura's foster father wasn't going to let a possible coincidence pass.

"Do you have any way to identify which Madden Eienno was your father, Niran?" he asked the young man gently. "I'm sure there have to be plenty in the country."

Niran's gaze fell. "I only have a picture," he admitted. "Of him and my mother."

Aura gasped. "I—I do, too!" she breathed, and her foster parents glanced at her in surprise.

"Well, why don't you go fetch it?" her foster father asked her finally, and Aura ran to do so.

When she returned, all doubts were dispelled. Aura's and Niran's pictures weren't exactly the same, but they were indubitably of the same couple. One difference was that in Aura's the two seemed younger, but in Niran's, Mrs. Eienno was carrying an infant—himself, Niran explained in semi-embarrassment.

"But I wouldn't remember any younger sisters if they were sent to orphanages," he continued. "My mother died before I can remember. You said you have a twin sister, Aura?"

"*Had*," Aura corrected him softly, flushing. "She died when Mom did."

"And you remember that?" Aura's foster father glanced at her in shocked amazement.

Aura nodded swiftly. "I remember since my memory began. It's strange, but I do. I remember my sister, and…and I remember my mother." Aura didn't want to go into details, so she quickly went on: "I don't remember ever seeing my father, though. Nor an older brother."

"This is fantastic." Suddenly her foster father rubbed his hands together excitedly. "Well, where are you staying, Niran?"

"I'm at the college just outside the city," Niran gestured vaguely. "I can't come into the city that much, however." He pulled a face. "Those college professors are strict. Don't go to college, Aura."

Aura was about to protest that she liked schoolwork, but her foster father addressed Niran before she could. "So do you think you can make it for Aura's birthday on Thursday?"

"Her birthday?" Niran grinned. "Thursday? I think I can."

"Come over for dinner, then," Aura's foster father urged, shaking the young man's hand. "I think she's having a party in the afternoon, so you can pop over earlier than dinnertime if you like," he offered.

"Thanks," Niran nodded. "I'll do that."

He turned, and glanced at the shocked Aura. "How old are you turning? Sixteen?"

"No—seventeen," she stammered.

Niran's green eyes sparkled. "That's right. Well, I guess I'll see you on Thursday, then," he decided, shaking Aura's foster father's hand again. "Thanks for having me."

"Any siblings or friends of Aura's are always welcome here," Aura's foster mother told him brightly. "Nice meeting you, Niran."

"You as well," Niran nodded, shaking her hand in turn.

He glanced towards Aura, but she seemed overwhelmed. So he smiled at her instead. "See you soon, little sister."

As soon as he was out the door, Aura grabbed hold of a chair to steady herself. "You—you said I'm having a birthday party?" she asked breathlessly.

Her foster parents glanced at each other, and then smiled simultaneously. "Do you want one?"

What Aura answered can be inferred from the fact that, the very next day after school, she was inviting Chanelle to her seventeenth birthday party on Thursday. Chanelle was excited at the prospect and promised she'd ask her parents if she could come.

"Oh, yes, and Niran wanted me to ask if this was yours," Aura went on, taking the small envelope out of her pocket and handing it to her younger friend. "He said he found it the other day after he was traveling with you and Jadelyn."

Frowning, Chanelle turned the envelope over, dropping the contents into her lap.

"I didn't think I dropped anything... Oh, this must be Jadelyn's," she realized.

Bending over to look, Aura immediately saw how she'd come to that conclusion. The item was a hair clip, in the shape of a *J*, decorated with stars. Probably some gift from her parents.

Aura sighed. "I guess I'll have to mail it to her, then," she decided, remembering the note Jadelyn had given her with her new address and the words *See you soon, Friend. Sincerely, Jadelyn.*

"Sounds good," Chanelle nodded, handing her the hair clip. Then she suddenly jumped up. "I almost forgot—I was supposed to rush home!"

Aura stood up, grinning. "Alright! I'll see you tomorrow! And then at the party on Thursday!"

"Goodbye!" Chanelle called after her, waving; and fled.

Aura stood up from the bench, shouldering her backpack and then walking slowly down the steps and out of the schoolyard, smiling. The sun shone down on her.

Eleven

VI

And then, when the time was right, the darker Darkness began to obliterate the brighter gray spots, one by one, discovering as it did so that its hypothesis had been correct. Where the greater Light had shone brighter before, now it became even more dim than it had ever been before. The brighter Light was still unaware of its purpose, its meaning. And after a brief, hopeful respite, the clouds over the world again began to darken, and the world sank into even deeper shades of gray than it had ever before experienced…

But not all the brighter gray spots were put out. Still a few remained loyal and alive. There was that one, original speck of brighter gray. There were others. And there was also the Twilight, the symbol of the world's past, blank gray. But even the Twilight was fading, into the darkest, eternal night of Death…

Twelve

The Twilight

"WHAT IS COLLEGE homework like?" Aura asked her newfound brother that Thursday. He had arrived before Chanelle, so Aura's foster mother had sent the two into the living room to get a start on Aura's homework.

Niran shrugged carelessly. "It does take forever, though," he admitted distractedly. "What about the high school homework?"

"You would know about that, wouldn't you?" Aura laughed. But Niran didn't know.

"I didn't go to high school here," he told her.

"I'd expect it's the same pretty much anywhere," Aura decided, glancing up as she heard her foster mother's voice from the kitchen doorway.

"Aura, do you know when your other friend is supposed to arrive?" Her foster mother looked anxious as she glanced at her watch. "She was supposed to arrive half an hour ago, wasn't she?"

"Oh, yes… I guess she was," Aura admitted, jumping up.

Her face was covered in confusion. "I did think I told her the right time."

Niran's green eyes were concerned. "I wonder if she ran into trouble."

"Mom, is it okay if we go to check up on her?" Aura asked suddenly, her red eyes lighting up. "She's only a few streets away. We can be back in five or ten minutes."

"That sounds alright, if you stay together, and watch out for traffic," her foster mother cautioned.

Niran stood up as well. "In that case, let's go, Aura!"

Aura felt safe walking with her older brother. The city was usually a dangerous place, which was why she had liked to walk to and from school with Eva, but with her brother she felt perfectly confident. And today was the best of days for such a walk. The sun was shining brightly, and the early spring birds chirping. The streets were clear of shadows and of any hint of darkness.

Today, she was different, too. Today Aura felt strangely alive. Her dark past was over, wasn't it?

But it wasn't just that. She felt strangely and powerfully alive—as if she could remake an entire world to be clean and bright like this one.

Laughing, she skipped along at Niran's side, who in turn was happy to see her looking so chipper. "Where to?" he asked her after they had gone a short distance down the street.

Cheerfully Aura pointed out the directions, and gaily they walked along. The world was at its brightest, the air at its freshest, the spring at its newest. Until they walked up the steps to Chanelle's family's home and saw that all the lights were off, and the window curtains drawn.

For the first time during that walk, Aura felt a sense of foreboding—as well as the sixth sense that someone was watching her.

She glanced around suddenly, but the only people around were in the street and no one was paying the slightest attention to the two.

Niran, too, seemed affected. "You're sure this is the right place?" he questioned, hesitating with his hand raised to knock on the door.

Aura had already glanced at the address.

"I'm sure," she returned, shivering as suddenly a cold gust of wind blew through them.

"Well, then," Niran shrugged, and knocked.

There was no answer. If it hadn't been for the suspenseful atmosphere, Niran and Aura might have walked away just then, but suddenly Niran wrapped his hand around the doorknob and pulled it open.

It wasn't locked.

Together the two walked down the dark hallway. Aura blinked as her eyes adjusted from the bright sunlight outside to the gloom inside, and suddenly she slipped her hand into Niran's.

She wasn't afraid, she realized with a sort of cold horror. She was…cold.

Suddenly, as they neared what must be the kitchen, Niran turned to face Aura, his face serious. "Stay here," he told her quickly; and then he tiptoed down the rest of the hallway, into the room.

Aura waited tensely, her heart hammering. *Now* she was frightened. What was wrong?

There was no noise from anyone but them, and she couldn't help but hear Niran's sharp gasp as he passed the threshold and then stopped. Aura's feet began moving of their own accord, and she ran over to him and to whatever he was looking at. Niran heard her, but too late.

"No, Aura, don't look!"

But she had already seen. Aura was frozen with horror.

Chanelle's entire family had been murdered; every one of them lay with the most terrified expression possible on their faces. They had somehow all been taken by surprise, without time to defend themselves. Aura couldn't see how they had been killed, and she didn't want to.

Her scream froze in her throat as she glanced up at the wall behind her younger friend's family, and saw something that shocked her almost more than the murders themselves.

The murderer had left a message, traced with what seemed a knife blade on the wall, but more so written in blood. Whose blood, Aura knew instinctively. But that wasn't the only horror.

"Face your fears"—how long can you look at the darkness around you?

"Chan…" The unspoken word died on her lips.

The world spun around her, then blurred away and became darkness. But not complete darkness; she saw the words that were written on the wall, except written in letters of black flame.

She saw the person she had seen in the truck that had crashed into Eva, except this time they were looking at her, with luminous, startlingly bright purple eyes. And smiling. No, smirking.

The girl was laughing at her, her face blocking out the words as she came nearer and reached out a black hand, blacker than even the girl's hair, with an eerie blue gleaming from it.

Aura couldn't move. This was worse than any of her nightmares.

Still laughing, the girl put her hand on Aura's shoulder, and suddenly Aura screamed. A piercing scream that dispelled the darkness and brought her back to her senses. The darkness, the girl, the words disappeared, and Aura found herself staring blankly into her older brother's face. It was his hand on her shoulder, not the dark girl's; but Aura was still screaming.

Her shoulders beginning to shake violently, she would have fallen forward if Niran hadn't been holding her. He knelt, and she fell onto her older brother, shaking in a nameless terror and horror she couldn't even describe.

Gently he wrapped his arms around her. She looked up into his green eyes, seeing there only a shadow of what she was feeling. But he, too, was shocked, and horrified, and afraid.

"Aura…" he whispered, and she tried to calm down. The scream died away into breathless sobbing, and she leaned back, against the wall.

Slowly Niran stood up. "Aura, I'm going to go for the police," he told her, his voice cracking. "You—"

"No!" Aura stood up, taking her brother's hand with a relentless strength. "You can't leave me here, Niran!"

Niran looked into her pleading red eyes that were filled with a child's fright. "Alright," he said finally. "You can come."

So she went with him to the police, and then back with the police, listening silently as he explained how he and his younger sister had come upon the scene. They were both interrogated, but it was obvious Aura was in intense shock and the police didn't ask her too much.

They did look at her suspiciously, though, Niran realized. Probably because the murder case of her former foster parents was still unsolved—Aura had explained the entire situation to him some days before. He knew their attitude was only to be expected.

But when one of them asked her directly where she had been half an hour before the supposed discovery, Niran couldn't help himself.

"We were at her foster parents," he answered before Aura could, and she glanced at him in surprise. Niran felt his cheeks grow warm as he went on, "She has an alibi for the entire day, since she went to school and up until now. I walked her home—I've been with her for hours!"

"And who are you?" someone asked him dryly; but Niran had enough presence of mind to give his name and address as well as explain that he was apparently Aura's older brother, which he hoped might clear up any confusion. It didn't change the situation much, and finally they were allowed to go home. Aura's foster parents had come to the station to pick her up, and she was still shocked and traumatized, but she did wave goodbye to Niran as she got into the car.

She was quiet the entire ride home, but her foster mother sat next to her, trying to calm her down.

"I'm sorry you had to see that, Aura," she told her multiple times. "They're going to find out who did it. It wasn't you, we know that. Don't worry."

Icy rain splattered on the windows and the windshield, and Aura's foster father drove carefully through the night. Aura was shivering, not just from the sudden cold snap. She couldn't stop thinking about Chanelle.

"Why?" Aura asked softly, when her foster parents tried to get her to eat something before she went to bed.

Her foster mother looked concerned. "You need to keep up your strength, Aura. Even if—"

"No, I mean, why would anyone hurt them?" Aura whispered, and her shoulders shook as she stared down into her untouched bowl of soup. "They were such a happy family," she continued, perhaps remembering how Chanelle's parents had invited Aura over for supper just a few nights before.

A single tear trickled down from her cheek and fell down into the soup, unnoticed. "I'm so afraid…"

The words died away into silence, until finally Aura's foster mother put her hand on their adopted daughter's shoulder. "What are you afraid of, Aura? We're your parents, you know. Don't keep secrets that can hurt you."

"No, I—" Aura began, then stopped, looking up into her foster parents' eyes for the first time since they had come home. In her own misted-over red eyes they saw something desperate, almost a kind of despair. "Was it because they were kind to me?"

"Of course not, Aura." Her foster father's voice was firm even as it was gentle.

"But Eva—and my old foster parents—" Aura's voice broke off.

"From what we heard, Aura, your old foster parents were not kind to you," the man broke in. Reaching across the table, he took Aura's hands, and held them.

Memories of a few, happy, former days flitted across Aura's eyes, and she whispered, "They were sometimes." Then, looking up and meeting the couple's gaze again, she continued. "I am afraid… So terribly afraid… You two are kinder to me than even my real parents were."

Suddenly she stood up, pushing her chair in carefully.

"Thank you for everything," she said simply, and left the room. Her foster parents heard her quiet footsteps down the hall, until they died away entirely as she entered her bedroom and softly closed the door.

Her foster mother stood up, but her husband shook his head, and she sat down again.

"She probably needs some time to herself." The man shook his head sadly. "The poor girl looks like she's seen a ghost. What if we were to take her on a vacation? I'm sure we can take her out of school for a few days; she has always had a perfect attendance record."

His wife nodded, sighing. "That's a good idea. A change of scenery will surely help her feel better. Oh, why do coincidences like these happen?"

"She doesn't seem to think it's a coincidence," her husband returned seriously. "Remember how I told you I was going to look more into her past? This girl we've picked up, her entire life has been a miserable one. I can see why she thinks it has a connection to her."

"But she's wrong," the woman protested sharply. "There is nothing wrong with Aura. All she needs is some light, and hope. She was so alive last week. So helpful and bright. Like an angel," she added thoughtfully.

Her husband stood up, as suddenly they heard knocking on the door. "Then we'll have to make her that way again. We'll take a vacation starting tomorrow, and then when school lets out we'll take her on a good, long trip. We'll bring back that spark in her eyes. But who would be knocking at this hour?" he finished, going over to the front door.

Though obviously he thought Aura's fear for her foster parents' safety was unfounded, he did take the trouble to look through the peephole before he unlatched and opened the door.

Two policemen stood there. "Does Aura Eienno live here?" they asked him, and slowly he nodded.

"What do you need?"

One of the officers took a deep breath. "To put it cleanly, sir, there's been another murder. Detective O'Leary, one of our detectives. We'd like to speak to Miss Eienno," he finished firmly.

Aura's foster father shook his head. "Now is not a good time. Aura is tired and—"

The policeman met his eyes. "Sir, this is urgent. We would like to speak to Miss Eienno immediately," he repeated, but this time Aura's foster father understood the command. He looked the policeman full in the eyes for a moment; then he lowered his gaze, stepping aside.

"Please sit down. I'll go get her."

He was back within a few minutes, Aura following him. She stopped in the kitchen doorway, glancing at the policemen; one of them gestured for her to sit down at the other side of the table, and she did so. She kept her hands on the table, twisting her fingers nervously.

"Sorry, Miss Eienno, but this should only take a few minutes," one of the officers told her pleasantly, glancing at the notebook he had in front of him. He looked back up at Aura, while the girl's foster father stood behind her chair, and her foster mother began to clear away the dishes from supper. "Miss Eienno, do you know a certain Detective O'Leary?"

She shook her head. "No."

It was obvious that the policeman had been expecting that answer, but it didn't do anything to relax the tension in the room. "He was member of the police force here in Coloni," the officer went on, still carefully watching Aura. "He was assigned the task of investigating the murder of your former foster parents, which included investigating you. He was satisfied with his investigation and informed us that you were innocent. Did you know that?" Aura was asked.

Another shake of her dark brown-haired head. "No."

The policeman smiled grimly. "Well, Miss Eienno, Detective O'Leary's body was discovered in his apartment, about an hour ago." His face remained calm and his gaze set on Aura as he went on, "His throat had been cleanly slit, and there were no signs of a robbery. The main article of importance that we found, Miss Eienno, was this. Of course, I only have a copy here with me, but it's an exact copy."

He reached into his pocket, holding up a piece of paper a moment later. It was from any ordinary kind of notebook, but the words written on it weren't quite so ordinary. Aura leaned forward to study them, and felt her face grow red as she did so.

Aura Eienno is the criminal, even if she doesn't know.

Aura's foster father had read the note as well. "What does this mean?" he demanded angrily. "You just told us that Detective O'Leary told you he was sure Aura is innocent."

"Apparently he changed his mind," the other policeman returned decisively. Looking straight at Aura, he informed her: "Miss Eienno, I would ask you where you were two hours ago, but for the simple fact that you were indubitably in the police station at that time. We would have taken this note to mean some other Aura Eienno—but it was *your* case Detective O'Leary was investigating at the time. We're going to continue our search for evidence. However, Miss Eienno, you are not to leave the city until further notice. Do you understand that?"

Aura's keen red eyes scanned his face one more time; and then she nodded stiffly. "Yes, sir."

A few minutes later, the policemen had left, but Aura still sat numbly. A small flame of fear flickered in her mind.

Could she somehow be murdering these people? And, which was even crazier, not know it herself?

Thirteen

VII

When the greater Darkness began its work, it set about striking its targets with swift, invincible, and deadly accuracy, building up a wall of fear and terror around the brighter Light. It destroyed even the Twilight. The darkness only grew, and so did the doubt and the despair. And soon it would be night.

Fourteen

Nightfall

AURA HAD HAD nightmares before, but she didn't that night—simply because she didn't sleep at all.

She didn't know what to believe. Could she somehow be hurting those who were kind to her? No…but if she wasn't doing it, it was someone who knew her very well—well enough to write "Face your fears" on Chanelle's family's living room wall.

But who? Who knew her? Who could hate her enough to murder all those close to her? Aura shuddered at the thought.

Suddenly, she half-sat up in bed, terrified for her foster parents and Niran. Gradually she calmed down, realizing that it was in the early hours of the morning and she was letting her imagination run away with her. The police were doubly on the alert that night. The murderer wouldn't dare to try anything, and if they did, they would be caught.

But who could it be? Aura told herself Detective O'Leary had to be wrong. It couldn't be her. Please, it couldn't.

She tried to think like a detective herself, and immediately her thoughts went back to her former foster parents' murder. It had seemed like a normal enough murder, though nothing had been stolen, but now as she thought about it Aura remembered that her former foster mother's face had been terrified, much like Chanelle's family's faces.

Then there was that truck that had hit Eva. Aura was sure she'd seen that person—especially as now she had seen it again since.

Suddenly she remembered the words she'd heard. *"Now do you know how I feel?"*

Aura tensed. Why would the person have randomly said that? Had Aura asked her how she felt sometime in the past?

For a normal person that might have seemed impossible to remember, who she had asked how they felt, but for Aura it wasn't that bad, what with her lack of childhood amnesia as well as her naturally good memory. She had grown up a loner, and hadn't talked to many people at that point besides her former foster parents and Eva. And obviously it wasn't them, unless her foster parents were haunting her—but no, Aura dismissed that thought immediately. Her imagination was definitely running away with her, wasn't it!

But if it wasn't her former foster parents, nor Eva… Who? It *couldn't* be Jadelyn. But had Aura talked to anyone else and gotten to the point of asking them how they felt…?

She closed her eyes, remembering. It didn't help that as soon as her eyes were closed all she saw was that face…that reminded her of her twin sister, and Kaja…

Suddenly Aura's entire body went tense again, and her eyes flew open. She had asked someone how they felt, and that someone had said—"You'll see."

Kaja!

Aura clenched her fists, breathing out slowly and sharply. She had no proof. Absolutely none at all, excepting her instincts and her memories. But she would confront Kaja tomorrow, at school. And the truth would come out!

But what if Kaja came for her foster parents in the night? As the possibility crossed her mind, Aura clenched her fists even tighter, then silently slipped out of bed. Kaja wouldn't take any more lives!

Her thoughts decisive, she sat down against the wall opposite her foster parents' room.

Her foster mother found her there in the morning, after nearly tripping over her. At first the woman was afraid something awful had happened, but then Aura woke up more and explained that she had been watching.

"But you're exhausted!" her foster mother exclaimed when Aura came into the kitchen some minutes later dressed in her school uniform.

"Huh? Oh." It was obvious the girl's thoughts were elsewhere. "I… I have to go," she told her foster mother distractedly. "To school, I mean."

Her foster father came in the room just then, and he went straight to the counter to make his coffee. "You said you were watching, Aura? What were you watching?"

"I was afraid," Aura told him simply. "I was afraid…someone would come."

Her foster parents didn't inquire further, but Aura went on of her own accord. "Mom, Dad… Please… Can we go somewhere after school?"

Her foster father glanced up, startled. "Aura, to tell the truth, I wanted to take you…us…on a vacation today. But then the police came last night…and you can't leave the city—"

"Oh, not out of the city," Aura broke in quickly. "Just… Can we go to the library?" she added. "Anywhere really."

The adults glanced at each other, and then Aura's foster father nodded. "Alright. We'll meet you there, then, after school—is that okay?"

Aura had a feeling that things would come to a climax when she confronted Kaja, and that she might not end up spending the entire day at school, but she nodded anyway. "Alright."

Even if she was expecting some kind of climax, Aura was not prepared for what she found at the school. The entrance was blocked off, and the crowd of her classmates didn't seem to have any idea why, but there were policemen standing there. Aura scanned the crowd quickly, but Kaja was not among them.

"Everyone, please go home," the policemen were saying. "Classes will resume tomorrow. Please go home."

"What's happened?" someone called out. "Why are there paramedics inside?"

Aura tensed. Paramedics? Someone had been hurt, or…?

"Return to your homes!" the policeman shouted again, but Aura hadn't stuck around to hear it. She was already going around the building and looking in the ground-floor windows. Guided by a strange sense of precognition, she headed straight for the window of her grade's main classroom.

Around fifteen of her classmates were being attended to by paramedics, but Aura saw at a glance that most of them had already been covered with white sheets, and the others were likely to end the same way.

Kaja was one of them.

Aura casually slipped closer to the large window, glancing through the room for anything she might have missed.

Then she saw it: more writing on the wall. Aura didn't have eyes for the policemen who were taking note of the words, only for the words themselves. Her name wasn't included, but whom else could they be for?

Can't you see that you are the Darkness?

Aura blinked and then looked at the words again, biting her lip. She, the "Darkness"?

But even as she wondered, she realized that it referred to the "Darkness" in the ancient legend.

Her?

That was just an old legend, she told herself; but the words of the legend still came to mind. Those spoken by the Creator.

"For your path is already set out for you. You will walk in the darkness and there will never be light. For in you is created, not Hope, but Despair. Not Light, but Darkness."

"No!" she screamed, holding her hands over her eyes. For a moment panic surged, but Aura told herself no, she was not the Darkness, the Darkness was just something out of the legend.

Someone knew way too much about Aura and her past and was trying to terrify her.

But why?

"It can't be Kaja," Aura murmured to herself, trying to use the process of elimination—and suddenly she froze. If it wasn't Kaja, then the murderer wasn't at school after all. And if the murderer wasn't at school...

Her foster parents!

Forgetting the scene she had seen through the window—she couldn't help anyway—Aura ran back around the school building.

But suddenly she felt a hand grab her arm, and she stopped short, wheeling around. Aura was panting, but as she glanced at the person who'd grabbed her, she saw it was Niran.

"Aura!" He, too, sounded like he'd been running. "There you are!"

"I have to go home now," she told him, her voice brusque even though she was relieved and glad that he was alright. "My foster parents—"

"I just called them," he told her. "They're going to meet us now. Instead of after school."

Aura's mind temporarily blanked out. "You what?"

"Listen, Aura," and Niran's hold on her arm tightened. "The police want you at the station now."

"I didn't do any of it!" Aura told him urgently, her red eyes flaming. "I don't know who is! But if they keep on the way they're going they'll be heading for my foster parents next—and—and you!"

Niran looked into her eyes a moment. Then he nodded slowly, and the two started walking down the street.

"I believe you," he told Aura quietly. "But do you know more than you seem?"

Aura was relieved that he was listening to her, but she was still trying to process.

"I don't know, Niran," she returned quickly. "I...I'll tell you as we go. Where are we going?" she added as an afterthought.

"Sorry, Aura... The police station," he informed her. "But we'll take the long way, and maybe we'll end up changing our destination. Don't worry about your foster parents, they're supposed to be on their way to the station as well. What's going on?"

Aura took a deep breath. "I will. I'll tell you everything, Niran—but I'm warning you, it sounds crazy, and I haven't got any proof."

"Tell away," Niran shrugged, sticking his free hand into his pocket.

For a couple of seconds they walked on in silence. Then Aura told him, "It all started when my old foster parents were murdered."

The rest of the story came out in a rush, and Aura really did tell her older brother everything, including her suspicions about Kaja, though obviously she had been wrong in that direction. She told him about the phantom girl in the truck that had hit Eva, and the words Aura had heard. She'd heard that voice again when she last told Jadelyn goodbye. Then the murders had started again.

She told Niran about her doubt and horrible fear that the last message might be correct—could she be the Darkness, or at least something to do with it?

But she was sure that whether it was actually herself or someone else, her foster parents and Niran would be targeted next.

"Because you three are…the only ones," she stammered, not knowing how to say it. Niran glanced at her eyes and saw the haunting there.

"I'm afraid, Niran," she whispered. "I can see death now, without being as traumatized. But you three… You are the only ones left."

She hesitated. "I…"

"You what, Aura?" her older brother asked her gently.

"I don't want you and my foster parents to die," she murmured, and there was real pain as she said it.

Her eyes blurred. Suddenly she glanced around. She thought she had heard something, but when she looked about her she discovered they were standing in an underground subway station. Aura was puzzled.

"Why are we here?" she wondered, and Niran smiled.

"We're not on the way to the police station anymore," he replied seriously. "We're on our way back to your house."

She squeezed his hand tightly. "Thank you, Niran!" she beamed.

But even as she said it she felt a sudden breath of air on the back of her neck, almost as if the wind was blowing.

But they were in an underground subway—there could be no wind.

As the thought crossed her mind, she glanced around again, this time seeing the shadow directly behind her and Niran. She tensed, and was just about to say something to Niran when she heard someone else whisper into her ear.

"What is there to hope for?"

And just then, Niran shrieked. As the words died away, Aura realized suddenly that someone had shoved him, forward, into the subway tracks. And the train was coming.

"Niran!" she screamed in a panic, reaching forward; but her hand came back instinctively as the train whistled by.

She was too late.

And then she fancied she heard that voice again. But this time it was laughing.

Aura glanced around, but no one around her was laughing as they ran over demanding if she was okay, what had happened to her friend, and so on.

Aura felt numb, but her mind was suddenly filled with one thought: her foster parents could even now be being targeted.

If they weren't...

If they weren't dead already.

Ignoring the people clamoring around her, Aura suddenly came to her senses and took off running down the subway tunnel. Maybe she realized subconsciously that it looked like she was running after pushing Niran onto the tracks, and maybe she subconsciously ran faster. But her whole being was focused on arriving home before it was too late.

She failed.

But the words on the wall...

Do you think I'll forget your other friend?

"Jadelyn!" Aura whispered. The word cut into her like a knife.

For a moment she was irresolute. What good could she possibly be now? She would arrive too late, like always.

But the hesitation lasted only a moment. Jadelyn was her friend—the best one she had. The *only* one she had. Aura had to try to save her, no matter how slim the chance.

Running upstairs, she found the note Jadelyn had given her, with her new address on it. Stuffing that into her pocket, Aura ran back down the stairs, and dialed the police from the phone in the kitchen. She left the phone dialing, and left the door unlocked as well when she left the house, trudging desperately on through the pouring rain.

Aura would have to leave the city to go to Jadelyn, which she wasn't allowed to do, but she didn't care. All that mattered right now was that she saved Jadelyn's life.

How, she didn't know. But she would find a way.

Outside the train Aura had boarded, the morning had turned gray. But even then it would still be hours before she arrived at her destination.

Fifteen

VIII

When the net closed, it closed swiftly. Night soon fell, and with the passing of the day passed also the last hope of the world's survival. However, that first brighter gray spot, which had guessed the greater Darkness's plan, managed to warn the brighter Light before it, too, was eliminated. And then could only follow the final battle…

But for the first time, the brighter Light was aware of its power. The darker Darkness's plan had been at least partially foiled. To defeat the brighter Light, it would have to fight, and win. It knew that Light is stronger than Darkness, Life is stronger than Death, and Hope is stronger than Despair. It would have to win before the Light became fully aware. Because then the battle would be over.

Sixteen

The Final Battle

AURA DIDN'T EVEN stop to fully investigate the crime scene at Jadelyn's family's house, only long enough to realize that Jadelyn was not there with her father, mother, sister, and brother. This time there was no writing on the wall—there was a note, however, obviously for Aura. It had been written quickly, in Jadelyn's handwriting. And it told Aura where her friend had been taken.

Aura called the police from Jadelyn's family's phone. Leaving the phone ringing again, she walked quietly out of the house of death into the streets of the city—then stopped to ask someone where "Poslebitva Castle" was. They told her, despite being probably startled by the desperate look in the strange girl's red eyes. Calling her thank-you as she left, Aura walked swiftly on. She knew Poslebitva Castle—an ancient, abandoned castle just a couple of miles out from the city.

Eventually, after about an hour of hard and fast walking, Aura found herself running up the outside stone castle steps as hard and fast as she could.

It was raining now, cold, icy rain that felt almost like hail. The wind blew in her face as she reached the top of the steps and looked about the castle ramparts in a panic.

The building had long fallen into ruins, but there were still plenty of places

Jadelyn could be. If she was even here.

Aura was suddenly filled with doubt.

"Jadelyn!" she screamed out, the wind whipping the words away from her almost as soon as they were spoken. It stung her face, and made her long dark hair swirl about her.

She listened for an answer—with one last spark of hope.

Then she heard her friend's voice: weak, but alive.

"Aura? Is that you?"

"Jade!"

Aura ran towards the voice with her last ounces of strength, and finally discovered Jadelyn. Her brown-haired friend was leaning against the short, jutted wall of the far ramparts.

Jadelyn raised her head as Aura came nearer, and Aura saw immediately that the front of her school uniform was drenched in blood.

She dropped to her knees at Jadelyn's side, whispering her name.

"Jadelyn… Are you alright?" Aura asked her helplessly, even though the answer was obvious. But she didn't wait for Jadelyn to respond before she slipped off her own uniform blazer, bunching it up and trying to stop the bleeding, even though she had no experience at all in the first aid field.

Jadelyn had already tried that, Aura realized—her friend's blazer lay beside her, completely soaked.

"Aura, listen…" It was clear that Jadelyn had been waiting, and bleeding, for a long time. She dropped her head forward again. "Do you…do you remember the legend?"

"The legend?" Aura murmured, then shook her head. "Jade, we have to get you to a hospital!"

She looked around despairingly, but they were far out from the city, on top of an ancient crumbling castle, and there was no one around for miles.

"Aura!" Jadelyn summoned the last of her strength, and leaned her head back so she could look at her friend's face.

She lifted one bloodstained hand and put it on Aura's arm, and Aura saw that she, too, was crying.

"Aura, please listen. The legend. You do remember it, don't you? I asked you to finish it."

"I—I haven't yet," Aura admitted, her own eyes blurring.

"That doesn't matter… Aura. Please believe me," Jadelyn whispered, holding her arm tightly. "You are the Light. Please… Live…"

Suddenly a thrown knife sliced the air between them, seemingly from nowhere, and Aura stared at her friend in disbelief as Jadelyn crumpled forward.

Gently she eased her friend to the ground. Jadelyn's eyes closed, then opened again. Her lips were moving, and Aura bent close.

"Live, Aura…finish the legend."

That was all she had time to say, before her blue eyes closed again and forever and she fell back limply. A strangled gasp escaped from Aura's throat, and she was choking on her tears.

"No…Jade!"

There was a footstep behind her, and then that voice, that Aura hadn't really expected to hear again.

"Well, I'm honestly surprised. I didn't think she'd risk it. Her loss."

Aura swung her head around, seeing the phantom girl for the first time. For a moment she was frozen immovable, but then she found she could speak.

So she did so, as she stood up slowly to face the girl. "Who are you?"

The girl smiled. "I am Kaja. Your twin sister."

Aura felt the world reel.

"But my sister is dead!" she shouted back, unable to control the tone of her voice. "And what about the real Kaja?

The phantom Kaja's voice, on the other hand, stayed level and cool. "She wasn't me; her name wasn't Kaja. She's our cousin."

"She was helping you?" Aura gasped out.

But the shadow girl shrugged.

"I was only using her," she replied derisively. "Like I used Eva…and Jadelyn…and *you.*"

Aura straightened her shoulders, still staring.

"How can you be my twin sister?" she demanded. "My sister is dead. You aren't her. You can't be, you—!"

Words failed her. There was nothing to describe the calm, cool, darkly transparent murderer with the glowing purple eyes.

"I never was alive," came the answer, and Aura started. "Because… I am Death. I am Darkness, and I am Despair. You were the Light, but you never realized, and so now you've lost it all, Aura."

Kaja took a step closer to Aura, who didn't move; and she lifted her hands slowly. A darkly gleaming blade appeared between them, and Kaja took it out of midair. When she wrapped her hand around it it began to glow a cold blue, like the clothes she wore.

Aura could only watch as she walked even closer, until finally she stood right in front of her sister, the dark sword raised on high.

"Do you realize now how I feel?" Kaja asked her softly, her eyes burning with hatred. "'You will walk in the darkness and there will never be light.' The legend was a true story, Aura—it just hasn't happened yet… And now it happens."

She smiled, an overwhelmingly horrifying, demonic smile. "Just remember that. Once upon a time…you were the Light."

Aura saw the sword coming down on her; she heard it whistling through the air, and she didn't move. Her entire life flashed before her eyes, and she saw then what Kaja had meant: she had most certainly walked in the darkness.

And even if she won now, there could only ever be darkness for her. Everyone she loved and who had been kind to her was dead.

Why was she still alive? To live in despair?

What *was* there left to hope for?

And in that moment, she almost did really despair.

But then Jadelyn's face drifted in front of her eyes. And she heard her friend's voice.

"You are the Light, Aura."

She hadn't *been*. She still *was*.

Aura heard herself panting as she leapt aside and dodged the blow. She ran backwards, along the ramparts that were only a few meters wide. Kaja came after her, dark and relentless, but suddenly Aura felt herself filled with an overwhelming desire to live.

She felt instinctively for a weapon, for a sword of her own. Even as she glanced wildly around, she sensed more than felt her eyes glowing redder than ever before in her life.

The color of blood.

And blood is the life of the body.

She felt truly alive, and endowed with a limitless power. The power of Hope, the power of Light, the power of Life.

And then it appeared in front of her, her sword. Though it shone so brightly that Kaja jumped back, Aura wasn't at all intimidated.

She reached out and took the sword by the hilt. The instant she touched it, she knew.

This weapon was hers. And she could use it.

Kaja struck at her then, but Aura deflected the dark blade with her own, and sparks flew. Again and again the two struck at each other, dancing a deadly dance on the narrow ramparts.

Aura and her sword shone with an unearthly light, and Kaja radiated a despairing darkness. Around them, the world was frozen. It was only the two left alive in a world of ice.

They fought on and on, until Aura found herself panting. She still felt her power. She could still use it. But unlike Kaja, she was human, and she was alive, and she knew that that was her only weakness.

Except Life wasn't a weakness, but she hesitated. What was the use of fighting a battle like this?

And then she realized that Kaja, too, was hesitating; but then the dark twin leapt forward with renewed energy, though she had lost her cool.

"You can't kill Death, Aura!"

Aura responded with a powerful, desperate blow that knocked Kaja's sword out of her hand.

"Where there is Life, Death cannot exist!" she screamed as Kaja fell to the ground, weaponless.

For a moment Kaja stared up at her, her purple eyes still fearless, but now Aura could see the despair in them.

Despair, Darkness, and—Death.

"Killing me will achieve nothing, Aura," Kaja hissed, and some of the blue radiating from her seemed to die away. "Life is dying. The world is dark. And hope is gone."

Suddenly Aura stopped, and threw her own sword away.

"No!" The word tore itself from her throat, in a voice even Aura had never heard before.

She threw her head back, and looked at the sky, and when she lifted her hands, lighting came down, lighting up the gloom around her.

It grew, and she couldn't see anything in the blinding light, but she could hear what she was saying, even though she only knew vaguely that she was the one saying it. She said it over and over again, as if it could somehow bring life to the cold, frozen, dead world.

"No, life cannot die! No matter how dark it is, I will not let it die!"

She remembered how her real mother had died, in the hospital so many years before, despairing. And how Aura's entire being, her very soul, had revolted.

"There is Hope still! There is Light, there is Life! There is always something to hope for! To *live* for!

"I will not let it die!"

And suddenly she became aware of a great calm around her, and the blinding light gradually vanished. It was raining again, she realized, as she sank down to her knees on the pavement of the castle rampart, exhausted.

But there was someone lying on the stones in front of her, and as Aura looked she recognized her twin sister again, but this time the glow was gone from her eyes, and the strange blue radiance had disappeared. The purple eyes were focused on Aura, and Aura realized suddenly that her twin sister looked frightened, and scared—and alone, so terribly alone, and little. The demon was gone, leaving only the girl.

"Kaja?" Aura whispered, tears blinding her.

"Aura," Kaja whispered back, and her own eyes filled with tears. She reached out a hand—such a white hand—and Aura took it, holding it. She saw that Kaja was fading, slowly but surely.

"Aura," Kaja repeated, and she sat up, holding Aura's hand tightly. "I…I'm afraid."

Aura threw her arms around her sister, realizing for the first time the full meaning of the legend. It wasn't fair, she thought bitterly; why should someone have to be created if they would only walk in darkness? If their destiny was to destroy or be destroyed? And she realized that the Darkness in Kaja had been destroyed, she had destroyed it, and there was only her little, twin sister who had never had a real chance at life.

"Kaja," she whispered again, sobbing. She felt her sister disappear, and she leaned back, staring at the shadowy frame even as that, too, disappeared. She was still holding Kaja's hand, but it was fading rapidly.

"I'm sorry," came a faint murmur from somewhere around her. Nothing like the terrifying voice Aura had heard before, but a quiet, sad, little girl's voice. "Live for me, big sister."

"You never had a chance!" Aura sobbed. But her sister's hand was gone, even if Aura still felt warm from the touch.

She stood up. Her red eyes were still shining brightly, but her long hair and clothes were soaked. Her face wasn't wet from just tears, though she was still crying. Aura stood there, looking out over the frozen landscape. Everything was dead and cold.

Turning, she caught sight of Jadelyn's limp form, and ran over to her. She had won the battle. Why couldn't Jadelyn, too?

"Jade!" she called out, and dropped to a kneeling position, leaning over her friend. Jadelyn's faintly blue eyes were still dim and lifeless, and her hands were cold. Aura took her friend's hands and held them, crying. Jadelyn was gone. And Aura was the only person left alive in the world.

"No, Jadelyn, don't be dead," she whispered to her.

The wind whistled around them, the rain poured, and the darkness covered everything, but Aura could still see her friend's white, cold face as she screamed out one, last word.

"LIVE!"

There was lightning again, but this time it was coming from Aura's hands, twisting around her, flooding out and into the landscape, lighting up the sky, lighting up the world. Aura fell back, still screaming as the light enveloped her and filled her with an unbearable, overwhelming pain.

And then it was over, and she was lying on the castle stones, her eyes closed. For a moment she wondered if she were dead; she realized her power, only just discovered, was now gone from her. But gone where?

She could feel the sunlight on her face, and she heard the birds chirping. Everything was so calm and peaceful.

Dawn, she thought.

Suddenly someone took her hand, and Aura's red eyes flew open. Her vision was blurry for a moment, but then she saw Jadelyn's anxious face above her, leaning down.

"Aura?"

"Jade" and Aura stood up. She didn't ask Jade what had happened. She didn't need to. Everything was bright and warm and sunny as she and Jadelyn hugged. The world had been relit.

Suddenly Jadelyn leaned back, laughing as she pointed behind Aura. "Aura, look!"

So Aura turned, and looked, and saw a crowd standing on the green, green grass by the base of the castle. Her eyes grew wide as she saw them.

Her foster parents, and her old ones too, and her real parents. Niran, and Chanelle, and Chanelle's family, and Jadelyn's. Even her classmates. Countless others that Aura didn't even know. And they were all smiling and waving to her. Aura caught her breath.

And Jadelyn caught her hand, and when Aura looked at her her friend's blue eyes shone with a sincerity that was even brighter than the sunshine. "You lived, Life!"

Holding hands, the two ran to the stairs, and then leapt down step by step together, towards the welcoming crowd. The clean, fresh wind blew in Aura's face. And the sun shone.

Seventeen

75

—

And so there was fought the final battle, until Light summoned the last of its power and destroyed Darkness completely. And with the greater Darkness, no darkness could stand against the brighter Light, and the world became alive, and hopeful, and full of light. Full of Life.

★ The End ★

About the Author

⚜

Gabrielle Marie Kozak is an American author whose fiction explores pressure, endurance, and the cost of refusing to surrender oneself to oppressive systems. Her debut, *The Trooper Series*, began as a body of work written before she graduated high school and introduced her recurring focus on individual sovereignty under strain.

The eldest of nine children, Gabrielle spent nearly two years as a religious sister before turning her attention fully to writing and publishing. Her stories center on those who carry responsibility, those who break beneath it, and those who survive when systems fail.

She lives in Nebraska and loves writing, coffee, and all things Poland.

Website: **gmariaek.com**

Thank you for reading!

If this story stayed with you, I would be grateful if you'd consider leaving a short review. Reviews help books like this find the readers who need them.

Your time, your attention, and your support truly matter.

If you'd like to continue reading my work, **The Trooper Series** is the best place to start.

Trooper A1: The Purple Blitzkrieg is the first book in the series.

Trooper A1: The Purple Blitzkrieg
SHE LOST HER BROTHER - JUST NOT THE WAY SHE THOUGHT.

Moira Whyte refuses to believe the **bloody evidence** that confirms her brother's death. Instead, she begins to hack into **Encephalon**, the underground network built to **subjugate the entire world.**

She's right. Her brother isn't dead.

He's worse than dead.

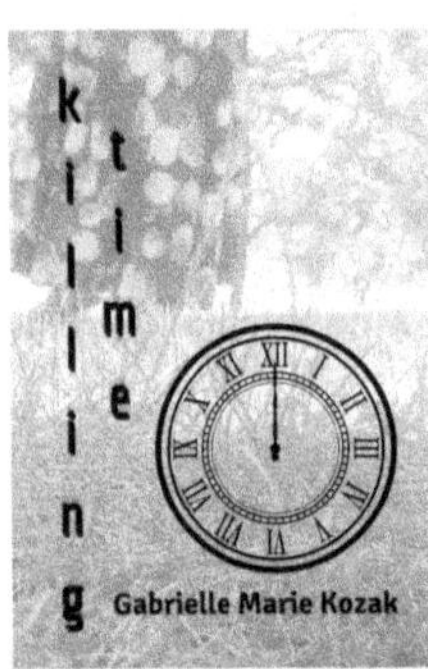

Killing Time

SHE'S ACCUSED OF BEING A SERIAL KILLER - WHILE THE REAL ONE IS HUNTING HER.

Pietro Dola thought his career was normal—until he walked into a hospital room with a team of police and saved the life of an orphaned teenager he was supposed to arrest.

Now he's asking the impossible question: how can Elvira Thyme be a serial killer... when the real serial killer is hunting Elvira?